IF YOU KISS ME

CIARA KNIGHT

If You Kiss Me
Book V
Sugar Maple Series

Cover art by Yocla Cover Designs
Edited by Bev Katz Rosenbaum
Copy Edit by Jenny Rarden
Proofreading by Rachel

Created with Vellum

READER LETTER

This book has a special place in my heart because it's all about second chances. Have you ever done something in your past that you regret? I know, who hasn't, right? Well, this story is all about second chances for a woman who made some terrible mistakes that cost her friends and family. Does she deserve forgiveness and love again in her life?

That has been the topic of every reader letter I've received since the first story, If You Love Me, was released. Well, this is what you've all been asking for, and I think you will be pleased with Jackie's story. I'm happy to report that early reviews are answering this question and I love every letter I receive.

I look forward to hearing from you about the conclusion for the first season of Sugar Maple. Let me know if you hope for more books in this series.

Sincerely,
Ciara

CHAPTER ONE

The green buds on the trees out in front of Jacqueline Raynor's small boutique in the heart of Sugar Maple took her back to spring in New York City. The place where she'd had a taste of living her dream. A dream she planned to return to as soon as she figured out how.

She ripped her gaze from the goings-on outside, paused at the mirror to fluff the side bow at her petite waist, and eyed her own knock-off of a Jona Silaki design.

How long had it been since she'd created an original? Okay, she'd worked on Mrs. Strickland's dress for her wedding, but it wasn't an original exactly. Mrs. Strickland had showed her pictures of exactly what she wanted, and Jackie had pieced it together. It didn't even garner any attention when Knox filmed the wedding as part of his coffee whisperer segment about Felicia.

She returned to her open laptop at the counter. The image of the capri pants and the sleeveless top in a pale blue gingham were close to Jacqueline's outfit but in green to show off her auburn hair and the waist set a little higher for a retro look.

Photos of fashion week cluttered the small screen with pops

of color, mixed patterns, and windswept hair. It was an event that had once ruled Jackie's everything. Front-row seating, exclusive parties and after parties, and after, after parties where she'd socialize with Wes Graden, Fernando Vici, and her favorite of all, Jona Silaki, not to mention the hundreds of other world-renowned designers. Everyone knew who Jacqueline was only two years ago, and they all wanted what she had to offer.

It hadn't been an easy life but a fast-paced, luxurious one that filled her with energy. Twice a year, she'd attend fashion week in New York, and then she'd fly to London, and then to Paris, even sometimes to Miami. In the end, she'd return prouder of her own designs, knowing that the best boutiques and shops around the world would fight over them. Well, they were her designs but with her ex-husband's label—Langford.

Everyone wanted her designs, even if they'd believed they were David's.

Until they didn't.

The front door opened, inviting a breeze to sweep through her shop, bringing the smell of fresh flowers, the sound of birds, and the unwelcome intrusion of one of her best friends turned enemy turned frenemy. She slammed the laptop shut before Carissa Donahue decided to overanalyze her researching fashion week. Despite Jackie's fall from fame—thanks to her ex-husband —she was still a designer. An underappreciated one in Sugar Maple, Tennessee, but still she was good.

So she'd thought.

"Hi. How's your morning going?" Carissa held a white bag from her Sugar and Soul Bakery and an undoubtedly perfect cup of coffee from their other friend, Mary-Beth Richards, who owned Maple Grounds. The last of their Fabulous Five high school turned grown-up friends to dive into the murky pool of commitment. Sure, Tanner McCadden was a small-town hero morphed into a football coach and farmer, so he was perfect for her, but why did all her friends have to get caught into the net of happily-ever-after-for-now? If they only knew what love brought later.

"I'm great." Jackie forced a welcoming smile, despite her wanting to be left alone to deal with her pathetic post-fashion-week life.

"Jackie, please. I know you better than that. You were probably looking at fashion week news, crying over the fact you weren't there. You could've gone, you know."

The idiocy of her words would take too much energy for Jackie to explain. How would Carissa ever understand being cast out of fashion society, only to return as a farm hound with fleas —unwanted and festering with failure. "My name's Jacqueline."

"Sure. So, Jackie. I brought you a new gluten-free, sugar-free tartlet that I thought you might like, and Mary-Beth sent you a non-fat, soy, something, something." Carissa plopped them both onto the counter and waited expectantly.

"You don't need to bring me sweets I won't even eat." Jackie had learned a long time ago that no real woman in New York City admitted to eating.

"Well, it's here if you want it."

Jackie tapped her sage-colored nails against the glass countertop. "Why are you being so nice to me? What do you want? You still hate me for stealing your fiancé back in high school." The words felt like acid on her lips. Her biggest mistake—no, sin —in life that haunted her daily. At the time, she'd convinced herself that she was saving Carissa from an unhappy ending and giving her an escape from small town life. A journey that ended before they had even reached the big city. Now that she was grown up and wiser and had her own heart broken, she'd spend the rest of her life trying to make up for that gross error in judgment.

"We've been over this. I'm not mad anymore. You did me a favor." Carissa nudged the bag toward Jackie.

"You should be." Shame filled Jackie until a snap of realization broke her self-loathing trend. "That's a bribery tart. Spill it, girlfriend. What do you want?"

Carissa toed the floor, her hair falling over her face, and Jackie wanted to chastise her for the way she'd let herself go already. Especially when she'd snagged the devilishly handsome man, Drew Lancaster, only a few months ago. Or had it been a year? "Wait, that's it. This has to do with your wedding, doesn't it?"

Carissa's face lit up like a girl on proposal night. "Yes."

"You want me to design and make your wedding dress." Inside, Jackie sang with the opportunity to do something nice for the friend she'd wronged so profoundly.

"Yes." Carissa leaned on the countertop, smudging the glass before she remembered better and shot up straight.

Was this only because Jackie's business had never taken off in Sugar Maple? "I don't need pity work." She stepped out from behind the glass separating them and straightened the latest summer dresses she'd created. "I listened to a friend of mine and designed for the small-town woman more than the big city girl."

"They look amazing. As a matter of fact, I want to get one. Do you have my size?"

"Sure, size frumpy is available." She couldn't help herself. Her pet peeve in life was being treated like a doll that had to be coddled or it would break. Besides, her friends never wore her clothes. They didn't like fine garments.

Carissa ignored the rude remark, but Jackie still wished she could pull it back into her mouth. Why she had to be so hostile all the time to her best friends and why they put up with it, Jackie wasn't sure. "I'll make your dresses. I guess Stella wants one, too. Are you two still thinking of a town square double wedding?" Excitement drove her to pull her special sketch pad from a drawer and open it to record the ideas bombarding her mind all at once.

"Stella said she's going to wear the white dress you gave her the night before she went on her first date with Knox."

The ideas dammed inside her brain. "Seriously? Does she even think about the fact that her fiancé is an internet sensation and he's about to do a segment on my store? No. This won't do. Tell her to be here after the shop closes one day this week for us to talk about this. She's only planning on wearing that dress to stick it to me because I tried to sabotage her first date with him." Jackie bowed her head at yet another example of her unworthy friendship shenanigans.

"You did tell Knox where to take her," Carissa said in a playful tone with the corner of her mouth curved up.

"Who knew she wouldn't enjoy the best date place in town?" Jackie shoved the sketchbook aside and returned to the summer dresses to finish straightening them on the hangers.

"You had him take her to a steak place when you know Stella is a vegetarian."

They both laughed at the idea of their abrasive car mechanic friend who lived in torn, stained clothing and combat boots dressing in a formfitting white dress and going to eat at a steakhouse.

"You know we all love you. We just wish you could love yourself," Carissa said in a soft, don't-kill-me-for-saying-it tone.

They stood in silence for nearly sixty seconds.

"Hey, I saw you with Elijah Warren the other day at Maple Grounds." Carissa picked up a hat and tried it on, turning side to side in the mirror. "How's that going?"

Jackie laughed. "You honestly think I'm interested in a hot bachelor fireman turned father of two girls and nicknamed Blaze? Me, the fashionista New Yorker who hates children? I think all that extra business you've had from your Knox Brevard internet segment is making you small-town crazy."

The door opened with a gush of fresh spring air. And if God himself could announce the entrance any better, Jackie didn't know how, because in stepped the ruggedly handsome, oh-so-wrong-for-her man. He was breathless and wore a furrowed-brow look of desperation and a front-of-fireman-calendar wet hair look.

Jackie needed a second to catch her breath from the shock of a man in her shop, so she returned to her safe spot behind the counter. Took a sip of her cinnamon and nutmeg–flavored latte and a bite of the tongue-tantalizing tart.

"Um, I thought it was your rule never to eat in front of people." Carissa gave a you-can't-hide-how-hot-you-think-he-is smile and removed the hat, hung it on the hook, and slinked to the door that Blaze held open with the charm of a southern gentleman. No man in New York ever made a woman feel as special as a southern man could.

Jackie swallowed the buttery pastry, doubting there was anything fat free or gluten free about it, and in a non-southern-lady way, she choked on it.

CHAPTER TWO

Instinct took over, and Blaze jolted into life-saving mode. He shot to Jackie's side. "You okay? Can you breathe?" He rubbed circles between her shoulder blades, but she continued to gasp, so he smacked her back several times. "Don't worry, I'm trained for this."

She coughed and choked, covering her mouth.

He stood behind her, wrapped his arms around her middle, and clasped his hands together.

She turned in his arms and slapped at him until he let her go. In between gasps, she said, "Trained to dislodge a tree branch from a three-ton elephant, maybe." Her watering eyes shut, and she took a sip from the to-go coffee before she continued. "I think you broke a rib."

"I hope you're not that fragile." He huffed and stepped back from the queen of mixed signals, ignoring that perfect blend of floral sweet and hidden secret perfume she wore. That was Jackie, the most mysterious and challenging woman he'd ever met. But he didn't have time for her games, not right now. Not when he was learning to care for two daughters who just landed on his doorstep a few months ago.

"Hardly." She straightened, her slender yet curvy frame in heels measuring a smidgen under his six-foot-two height. He found himself stretching his head a little higher.

"Are you going to stare at me all day or tell me why you barged into my shop, caused me to choke, and then tried to kill me with your brute force?" She half smiled that intriguing, mesmerizing, I've-got-a-secret kind of smile that drove him crazy. Correction, used to drive him crazy. Now he behaved like a grown-up who focused on family duties, not pretty women.

"Yes." Blaze thought back over what Knox Brevard had told him at the Ms. Horton and Mr. Strickland wedding last fall at the McCadden Farm. *Flattery will get you everywhere with Jackie.* "I know that you're a world-famous designer and that you're way too busy for a desperate father in need of a perfect formal dress for his daughter, but if you could find some time to help, I'd more than appreciate it."

She popped one hip out, causing the fluffy bow tied at her hip to flutter, drawing his attention down to her tiny waist.

"Eyes up here, you know." She snapped her fingers at him. "I don't know. A child's dress? Girls don't appreciate high fashion. She'll probably go make mudpies while wearing it."

"Mud pies? She's not four." He cleared his throat and softened his tone to a decimal below flattery but above desperation. "Besides, all my eldest daughter has talked about since coming to Sugar Maple is how she'd love to own a Jacqueline Langford–Just Jackie design."

"Raynor," she said flatly with an angry crinkle of her nose. "I design under my maiden name now."

"Right. Forgot that you told me that." He couldn't imagine what insane man had let a woman like Jacqueline slip away. A woman who would be able to keep Blaze's attention for decades, unlike the normal women he dated, in whom his interest fell by the main course. Not that she was sweet or possessed the southern charm of the usual girl in Sugar Maple, but she was fiercely independent, successful, and driven. Everything opposite of his ex-wife, who needed her hand held through life.

"And as for the store being called *Just Jackie,* a convenient mishap with the sign from a friend compiled with a town business license issue. I plan to change the name."

Blaze didn't care about the store name. He just needed a dress. "Listen, all Tabitha does is talk about you, and since I might have made a…what did she call it? Right, epic NeoRent mistake, I apparently need to make it up to her big-time."

"Why?" Jackie crossed her arms over her chest and tapped those deliciously high heels.

"What?" He searched for answers on her blank face.

"What did you do, and why do you have to make it up to her?" The way Jackie flipped her hair and waltzed to the center of the shop told him that she was enjoying this. But no matter how he felt about her, he was embarrassed to reveal the dumb mistake he'd made with Tabitha that had led him here. She was the only one in town who could score big with his daughter, and he needed a big win.

After careful analysis of his options, he decided he had to tell her what she wanted to know if he wanted to win this argument. Certainly she'd take his side about a dating issue anyway. "Apparently telling a boy not to touch my daughter or I'd have him arrested was some sort of a problem to a teenage girl."

Jackie tsked. "No, tell me you didn't."

The way she looked at him made him feel like a bad toddler who should be sent to his time-out mat. "I did."

"Tell me it was only in front of your daughter and not in front of friends."

He ran his thumbnail along the caulking at the edge of the glass top. "It might have been in front of the entire freshman class of Sugar Maple High School. Still don't know why that's so wrong."

Jackie smacked his hand. "Don't do that or I'll make you fix it."

She shook her head at him. "You wouldn't think there was something wrong with what you did, would you? I'm starting to see where NeoRent came from."

"What does that even mean? I don't understand half the things my teenage daughter is saying to me." He scrubbed his stubbled chin, remembering he needed to shave before reporting to the firehouse that evening.

"Neanderthal Parent. And that sounds about accurate for someone like you." Jackie waved the air, dismissing him like he was one of her fashion assistants. "Why do you care so much that she's mad at you?"

"Because she keeps threatening to call her mother and beg her to come get her." He clenched his jaw at the idea. He'd fought for custody from day one when she'd walked out of his life for another man with their daughters in tow. She'd been malicious and twisted drinking with his buddies into full-fledged alcoholism until he was only allowed supervised visitation. And then when that guy ran off because he'd been so exhausted with her theatrics, she came running back. That's when things really got ugly. Lies to her wealthy parents with lawyers combined with the allegations of his drinking and womanizing, and he was lucky to see his girls once a year after she moved them halfway across the country for the next guy. He'd backed down only when he saw the toll it was taking on his baby girls. Their mother loved them, and he knew she'd care for them. It was him she hated.

"Maybe she should. Did you ever think you weren't meant to raise two little girls?"

A flicker of resentment ignited in his gut. More because she was right than he cared to admit to himself.

"All the time, but I can't send them back. Their mother doesn't want them. After I fought for over five years for custody and then gave in so the girls weren't used as pawns in a custody battle, she now has a new man in her life and doesn't have time for her daughters anymore."

Jacqueline's lips and cheeks softened for a moment, but then she straightened some clothes and her shoulders stiffened once more. "You don't have room to judge a woman for wanting to date. You're a firefighter who has the name Blaze because you set women on fire when you look at them. Isn't that what the guys at the firehouse say?"

"No, that's not why." He rubbed his forehead. "Tell me that's not what they're telling people."

"If that's not why, then tell me how you got that nickname."

He pressed his lips together and thought about it for a moment. "No. It's too embarrassing." He threw his hands up in the air and strutted to her side. "I'll pay you for the dress."

"You can't afford one of my dresses on your salary."

He wanted to argue the point but decided it was most likely true. "I'm a great carpenter. I can make new shelving along the wall over there and build in window boxes for displays."

"That's something. But I want more for a Raynor original."

His heart fell, knowing he couldn't afford much between the live-in nanny on nights he had to stay at the station and the increase in electric, water, clothes, and food.

"I tell you what. As part of your payment, you have to tell me why you're nicknamed Blaze." Jackie crossed her arms over her chest, and Blaze knew she wouldn't let him out of telling him, so he might as well get it over with.

"Because, when I was a probie, I ran into a burning building to save someone."

Jacqueline's right eyebrow rose. "That doesn't sound so bad."

He thought about leaving the conversation there at half the truth but decided that if she found out the entire story later, he'd never live it down with the men. "I forgot some equipment and ended up trapped and had to be rescued."

She burst out laughing to the point of a snort. She quickly stopped and covered her mouth with wide eyes. He preferred the snort over uppity giggle she usually did. But either way, he wasn't going to stand there and be laughed at all day. He had things to do.

"Fine, you've had your laugh. Now what about the dress?"

"Bring Tabitha by this evening. I'll take her measurements and figure out what she likes. Don't worry. You'll get Dad of the Year, maybe even a hug in private from her."

The thought of winning his daughter over sounded like an impossible dream. "Thanks. I'll bring her by then."

He looked at his phone and realized he'd have to find someone to cover for him again. This would be worth it, though. With the plan in place to win his eldest daughter, he eyed the bakery, the coffee shop, and every other store in the town square for a way to connect with his youngest. But how could he connect to Charlotte when she had refused to speak since she'd arrived in Sugar Maple?

CHAPTER THREE

"I call this Fabulous Five operation wedding planning to order." Mary-Beth Richards, owner of Maple Grounds who was floating on a second-chance romance high, settled at the bistro table with the I'm-stupid-in-love grin that matched the rest of Jacqueline's four friends. Ugh. Why did love have to make people obnoxiously happy?

Sure, Jackie was happy for them, but it was easier to be supportive at a distance. Stella grunted, but even she looked like an abrasive, attitude-tossing mechanic turned candy striper.

Jackie pulled out her notebook to review her list. "First order of business is to address Stella's lack of appreciation for her fiancé's fame," Jackie said.

Stella grunted, but if Jacqueline didn't know better, she'd swear Stella wanted the big wedding. "Knox says he doesn't care if we have a big ceremony on camera or not."

"Honey, I think he probably said that to give you a way out." Felicia retrieved a folder from her bag that had no doubt been organized by her own ex-con-turned-innocent boyfriend. "I've brought some floral ideas with me that I think will make your wedding less flowery and more sophisticated. But I have an idea on how to incorporate Carissa's sweet side, too."

"How on Sugar Maple's famous tree are you going to do that?" Jacqueline asked.

"We will have two aisles instead of one through the town square. One aisle decorated for Stella and the other for Carissa. At the gazebo, we'll do simple garland and some painted leaves handwritten by the grooms and brides."

Carissa gasped, obviously caught by the idea since her own Drew Lancaster had tar and southernized himself. Jacqueline could still see the maple syrup dripping down his fingers with handwritten notes stuck to his clothes, face, and shoes. What a spectacle he'd made of himself. All because the mischievous town elder, Davey, had convinced him that was the only way to earn the town's respect. Jacqueline still believed that her elder friend had done it years ago, and that's why he'd tried to make another man humiliate himself. Not that Davey would ever admit it to the world.

Stella shrugged. "I might be persuaded to do this for Knox. Jackie's right—"

"Whoa, what?" Jacqueline dropped her hand to the tabletop with a loud clang.

"Don't make an epic deal out of it. You said I should appreciate Knox's position if I'm to make our marriage work. Well, this is me working." Stella adjusted her faux leather jacket and scooted her combat boots out to lean back in the chair in her it-doesn't-mean-anything posture.

Jacqueline picked up her non-fat, almond milk latte; she still couldn't comprehend how Mary-Beth made it taste so delicious. "Fine. Then let's talk dress."

Stella shot up, but Carissa turned to face her, taking her hand. "Remember, it's for Knox, right? You need a dress that people will want to own." Carissa tilted her head a smidgen toward Jacqueline. Realization attacked like a dozen cottonmouths that swarmed around her in the lake. No way was she getting bit. "That's why you came to the store to speak to me. You think that if I make your dresses and it goes well, my business will take off and I'll want to stay here. Let me be clear. There's no way that you or anyone else will ever get me to remain in this town. I'll return to New York when the time's right."

They all sat silent with downturned, unbelieving gazes.

"It'll happen," Jackie insisted

Felicia, the negotiator of the bunch, cleared her throat. "Of course it will, but think about using this as an opportunity to gain favor beyond your ex-husband, showing the world that you're worth ten of him with your amazing designs."

Dang, that girl was good. "You sure you didn't study psychology in college?"

Felicia only snickered and hid behind her own coffee cup.

"Fine, I'll do it to stick it to my ex-husband and as a gift to my two friends." She couldn't help but study the tiny chip on the mug's handle, unable to face Carissa.

Stella stood, eyeing her watch. "Fine. If you need to make an apology for stealing her high school sweetheart and we can all finally move on, I'm in. But let me be clear. No ruffles and no lace."

"Do you think so low of my design skills?" Jackie huffed.

"Design skills, no. Pulling a stunt, yes."

Jackie rose from the table. Mary-Beth snagged her mug and slid it into her protective personal space, as if Jacqueline would toss it at Stella. "I would never pull a stunt when it comes to a wedding dress. You have my word."

Stella eyed her with a narrowed gaze, but then the corner of her mouth twitched and her cheeks softened. "Okay, let me know when you want me to come by to work on the dress. I'm in." She toed the ground as if wiping away a smudge her boots had left on the hardwood floor. "Thanks."

Before anyone could react to the rare sighting of the congenial moment from Stella, she bolted out the door and to her old Chevy she'd restored with the help of Knox and his financial support. The car she'd held on to that had belonged to her abuelo all those years ago. That had to be the reason Knox won over the cold heart of Stella and softened her edges. He'd been the first man to ever treat her well since her grandfather.

Mary-Beth stood, clearing the empty mugs at the sight of Tanner McCadden coming by for his afternoon cup and kiss before he headed to the farm to work the day away. Why he didn't hire more help instead of working hard was beyond Jackie's comprehension. Perhaps he was waiting for his brother Hawk to return so they could work the land together. That was, if his brother decided to leave the military to come home to an old family farm.

"We'll get out of your way. Besides, I have to be back at the shop in about twenty minutes," Jackie said.

Felicia gathered her folder before Jackie realized they hadn't even looked at her arrangements. "That's right. I heard you're going to help with the spring formal at Sugar Maple High School."

"I'm what?" Jackie laughed at the absurdity of it. "I think the Sugar Maple gossip line let you down. I'm simply making a dress for one of the girls."

"Blaze's eldest daughter. Right. Well, she told the school that you'd also be helping with the planning of the event."

Jackie fumed. No way she'd be roped into doing some high school dance for Blaze's little girl. No matter how he smiled at her. She'd never agree to such a thing. The days of a man fooling her into bad decisions were dead, buried, and a two-hundred-year-old Sugar Maple had grown from the rot. "Again, I think you're mistaken. Who told you that?"

Felicia held her folder to her chest and headed for the door to escape. "I'm on the planning committee. We had a meeting this morning, and they asked me why you weren't there."

"You can let them know I'm doing no such thing. Got it?"

Felicia nodded. "Got it. There's only one small problem with that."

"What's that?"

The door opened with Tanner flashing the small-town football smile at everyone, and Felicia took her escape route with only a quick sideways wave and a few parting words. "I told them the entire Fabulous Five would love to help."

Jackie shot out the door after Felicia. "Wait one minute. Why would you say that?"

"Because the theme of the dance this year is Small-Town Royalty. And, hon, the Fabulous Five is royalty in this town."

Those words caught Jackie off guard, and she stood on the front walk with her mouth open until Davey shuffled up from the senior bus for their afternoon town visit.

"Looks like Jackie fell off her catwalk," he mumbled to Ms. Hughes, Felicia's grandmother turned fiancée to Davey. Apparently some fifty-plus-year romance had finally taken hold. Ugh. Jackie needed out of this crazy town and its obvious Cupid epidemic. No way, no how, would she ever let one of those wayward Sugar Maple arrows pierce her plans for a future far beyond her hometown. It was time to make a move, and if designing the wedding dresses for Carissa and Stella for the Knox Brevard show was her ticket out of here, she'd pay for it. Whatever it cost.

CHAPTER FOUR

The school parking lot was empty except a few teachers' cars, revving Blaze's stress. Why hadn't Stanley been on time to cover for him at the station for a lousy two hours? He jolted to a stop, flew from his truck, and raced inside Sugar Maple Elementary School. Inside, he found his two daughters huddled together on the floor.

Tabitha slung her bag over her shoulder, helped her baby sister up, and stormed toward him. "You're late. Again."

That expression was the best interpretation of his ex-wife's I'm-about-to-explode snarl.

"I'm so sorry, but you'll be happy to know that I'm taking you straight to Jacqueline Raynor's store for her to personally design a spring formal dress for you."

Tabitha sparked like a super-nova, but then a black hole swallowed her brightness. "Right, well, guess we're late for that now, too."

"Mr. Warren, I need to see you for a moment please."

Blaze recognized old Susan Miser's voice with its grizzly tone. "Yes ma'am."

Tabitha double huffed, but Charlotte remained silent at her

side. She hadn't muttered a word since she'd arrived here. "We don't have time for that now."

"Ms. Warren, I assure you that whatever frivolous plans you have are not more important than your sister's education." She waved for Blaze to follow her. "If you please."

He glanced over his shoulder at his girls, who remained huddled by the door. "It shouldn't take long. I'll be right back. Wait here."

He entered the classroom with the small desks and Ms. Miser's big attitude, not sure if he was more nervous about what could be wrong with Charlotte's work or just plain nervous at being back in the English classroom that he'd nearly flunked in fourth grade himself.

"Sit."

He eyed the small chairs and pointed at his big frame and looked questioningly at Ms. Miser. Based on her lowered silver-rimmed glasses and downturned gaze, he figured he best comply. "Yes, ma'am." With a deep breath held in, he squeezed into the desk and stretched his legs out in front of him, ignoring the seat cracking under his weight.

"Mr. Warren. I realize you're a relatively new father and that you work all hours, but these young girls should not be left to their own devices."

Blaze shot up straight. "My girls are never left unattended. I'm home or the nanny is home at all times."

She cleared her throat, obviously letting him know not to interrupt her again. "In broken homes, with a father working all the time, young ladies will search for attention anywhere they can find it. In this case, Charlotte has decided to search out negative attention by refusing to open her book in class."

He gripped the edge of the desk. "I see. Well, I will speak to Charlotte. I'm sure she will be happy to open her book in the next class. If you'll excuse me. I don't want to leave my girls unattended in the school hallway for too long. Good day, Ms. Miser."

Before she could spew more judgement his way, he hurried out of the classroom to find the girls gone. His pulse beat against his neck faster than his booted feet could carry him. Outside, he spotted Tabitha and Charlotte leaning against the truck. They looked tiny next to his oversized expanded-cab. Charlotte's mouth opened, and she said something to Tabitha.

"You spoke?" Blaze took three steps at a time and landed on his knees next to his youngest daughter, excited to hear her voice for the first time since she'd arrived back in Sugar Maple, but she smushed her lips together so tightly, their pink disappeared completely.

"Let's go." Tabitha took Charlotte by the hand and dragged her to the passenger door.

Deflated, Blaze stood and opened the door, and the girls climbed inside for a silent ride to Jacqueline Raynor's shop. Hopefully, this would win him some major dad points and he'd finally have some peace in his home again.

Once at the shop, he eyed his watch, realizing there wasn't much time to get them fitted and then home to the nanny before he had to return to work, so he ushered them out of the truck and then inside. "Hi, Jacqueline. We're here."

She nodded but continued with two customers. Charlotte collapsed onto some plush chair in the corner while Tabitha perused all the merchandise. She held a too-adult dress up to her chest in front of a floor-to-ceiling mirror.

"Nope, no way. You can ask for Ms. Raynor to design a dress for a fourteen-year-old, not a forty-year-old."

"You're so old-fashioned. If Mom was here, she'd let me have it."

Great. The "mother raises us better" topic he knew so well in such a short time. "Well, she isn't here and I am."

Jacqueline brought over her laptop and set it down on the table. "Take a look through these and give me an idea of what you like."

His phone buzzed with a message from Stanley. *Family emergency, need you to cover for me.*

He let out a long breath. "Sorry, girls. We'll need to do this another time. I've been called into work. I'll call the nanny now. We better get going."

Tabitha lifted her chin high into the air. "I'll take care of Charlotte and myself tonight. We don't need a nanny."

"No, watching out for your baby sister is my job. You're not the parent. We need to go."

Tabitha crossed her arms over her chest and dug in as if she wouldn't be budging until he physically moved her. That would only prove he was a NeoRent.

When he didn't move, obviously Tabitha realized she wasn't getting anywhere, so she approached Jacqueline. "I told everyone at school you'd be designing my dress. I wouldn't want someone from the high school posting about you letting a little orphan girl down to affect your business."

"Tabitha. Stop." Blaze hovered over her with the look that normally made men back down and run from him. "You will not blackmail someone into doing something for you. And you're not an orphan. You have me."

"It's not blackmail, it's extortion, and all I'm saying is that I want to help Ms. Raynor achieve her goals and would never want to harm them. I wouldn't start the trending, but you obviously don't know how high school girls work." Tabitha looked up at him with his same intimidating stare. "I wouldn't have a chance. The school would post the second they found out. It would be to ruin me because they are picking on the new girl, but instead it would harm Ms. Raynor, and I personally wouldn't want that. She's my favorite designer."

Jacqueline stepped forward. "I'll give them a ride home after we meet. Go ahead to work. I've got this."

"You don't know anything about children. You don't even like them." He blinked at her, trying to decipher her game plan.

She chuckled, a lighthearted, I've-got-this kind of sound. She was fearless about everything, even children. "And you do?"

He looked from her, to Charlotte, and finally to Tabitha.

"And you do?" Tabitha tapped her foot at him mimicking Jacqueline.

He wasn't going to tolerate any more disrespect out of Tabitha. "You go sit with your sister while I talk in private with Ms. Raynor."

Tabitha and Jacqueline looked at each other as if he was wasting both of their time, but she followed his orders and retreated from her teenage defiance. He cleared his throat and took Jacqueline by the arm, leading her to the fitting room and pulling the curtain tight. He hadn't realized how tight the space would be. They were practically touching chest to chest. He cleared his throat and pushed his back to the wall. "Um, listen. I'm doing my best here, but it's apparently not good enough. Tabitha has been angry since she arrived, and Charlotte hasn't spoken. I mean, I just got called into the sixth-grade language arts teacher's classroom."

"Not Ms. Miser." Jacqueline shivered. "She's the most hated elementary school teacher ever. Not because she's a horrible person but because she expects the best from her students and nothing less will be tolerated. That's why she despises the Fabulous Five. Stella altered her engine one time when the woman called me a diva." The way Jacqueline's eyes sparkled, she almost looked like a real girl, not this perfect mannequin he'd found in the shop. "I was being a teenage girl that demanded attention, so she kind of had a point."

"I need to get Charlotte to participate in class, or I don't know what the woman will do." He leaned his head against the back wall. "Listen, I don't know what you hope to accomplish here, but I promise not to let Tabitha create any trouble for you. I'll take the girls home with me now under the promise you can meet with her Saturday morning. I have off for seventy-two hours come Saturday."

"No," she said before picking lint off his uniform shirt.

"What?"

"No. Trust me, I can handle your little manipulative fashionista."

"How are you going to do that? I've been trying to figure out how to help her acclimate for weeks. All I get is hostility."

"Because I *was* her. Now go." Jacqueline swung the curtain open, and Blaze caught sight of Charlotte saying something to Tabitha.

He rushed out of the small space and to Charlotte's side. "You spoke. I know you did this time."

"No, she didn't," Tabitha announced before she stood and pointed to the door. "You're going to be late for work. You best go, Daddy."

Daddy?

"No. I saw her talking to you." He looked at his youngest daughter. "Talk to me." Blaze knelt in front of Charlotte, but she didn't speak. "Tabitha, can you get her to talk?"

"No. I'm not the parent, remember?"

CHAPTER FIVE

Tabitha whirled around the store holding up different outfits to her tiny, barely high school frame. It was nice to have someone so enthusiastic about her designs.

"This empire waist is nice, but not tea length. I want mini-skirt." Tabitha rubbed back and forth way too high up her leg with a karate chop hand.

"And what would your father say about that?" Jackie knew this spitfire would be the death of Blaze. The man had no idea what teenage girls were about.

"NeoRent doesn't know about fashion. If you tell him it's right for me, he'll let me wear it."

Jackie held up a tiara and waved it about like a little girl hypnosis device. She knew right then and there how to handle the girl, considering Jackie was once that age and knew how to speak her language. "Now you listen to me, young lady. Your tricks and terror may work on your father, teachers, and anyone else you come across, but it won't on me. If you want me to design your dress, you sit down and behave like you appreciate what I have to offer. You will not demand or order me around, but you may request changes."

Tabitha blinked at Jackie as if she'd grown two tiara-wearing heads, but then Tabitha's shoulders dropped and she settled into a chair at the glass table with green leaf pedestal. Jackie took her sketch pad and her notebook and joined Tabitha. She started a new list for Tabitha's dress. "So you like the empire waist. You have petite shoulders and a long neck, so that will be pretty on you."

"That's what I was thinking." Tabitha's eyes went wide with excitement. Jackie was glad they agreed on something. Jackie sketched the bodice in a pale blue.

"Not that color, though, right?" She rose an eyebrow but with less hair flip than earlier. "I mean, that's something for a little girl. Despite what NeoRent thinks, I'm not a child anymore. I'm a woman. Less princess, more sophisticated."

"I thought blue would go well with your skin tone and light hair." Jackie leaned back, reassessing her first thoughts.

"Black. I want something more mysterious, sexy."

"Sexy, huh?" Jacqueline forced her laugh to remain inside and eyed her drawing pencils and the various colors, deciding blue was still the right tone but perhaps darker—navy. "What's his name and how old is he?"

Tabitha's mouth dropped open. Her rosy cheeks flushed.

"I can read you because you're me. A younger version but with a father who cares."

"Promise not to tell my dad. Last thing I need is NeoRent barging into the middle of class and pulling the guy out by his hair." The pupils in her eyes went ohhh-so-cute large. "He has great hair."

"I tell you what. You behave like a young lady, and there's no reason for me to tell him. Let me guess. He's a senior, star soccer player, and tends to have young ladies drool over him."

"Football."

The realization of the one-word answer almost made Jackie lose her composure, but she knew that would only put up the young girl's walls. Not to mention making Andy forbidden chocolate mocha with a double shot of bad boy. Tabitha didn't need another person judging her. Not when the world was so judgy, especially the high school world. "What's his name?" Jackie asked, even though she already knew. How could she not? Mary-Beth's little brother was the star of Sugar Maple, and if Tabitha was anything like Jackie, she would settle for nothing less than the best, most beloved man around.

"Andy," Tabitha breathed more than spoke. "He's not just handsome, though. He's like…nice and smart, too."

"Yes, I know." Jackie took the navy pencil in her hand and returned to the bodice and straps of the dress.

Tabitha shot up, tucking her knees under her. "You know him?"

"He's the little brother of one of my best friends, so yes, I know him." In that moment, Jackie knew she could get anything from the girl.

"Seriously? Wow. Can you like hang with me or something so I can see him outside of school?"

Jackie eyed poor little Charlotte sitting alone in the corner kicking her feet back and forth. She reminded Jackie of Stella after that horrible incident where her father tried to sell her for drugs when she was a kid. Jackie had been too young to understand that Stella's silence meant something, but she knew now and wanted to make sure this little girl was okay. "I'll think about it if you tell me one thing."

"What's that?" Tabitha bounced on her knees as if she'd launch from the chair at any chance to see Andy Richards.

"Tell me why your sister won't talk." Jackie swallowed, scared of the truth but knowing she had to help if she could. "Did something bad happen?"

"Yes. I mean, no. It's just that she doesn't trust adults much. Not the ones who say they love us and want to care for us. Dad bolted when we were young, and now Mom wants a man more than us so she shipped us here." Tabitha shrugged. "You can't blame her. Sometimes I wish I could get away with not talking to adults."

"No, you can't blame her. Life can be complicated. It's hard for me to believe your father abandoned you, though. He mentioned something about losing full custody of you, but something tells me he wasn't happy about it."

Tabitha double shrugged. "Don't know, but if Dad tries to make her open that book in class, he's going to push her away more. He doesn't understand."

"Can you explain it to him?" Jackie rotated the sketch, keeping her eyes on the task at hand, scared that eye contact might break their moment of conversation.

Tabitha leaned into her, looking over her shoulder at Jackie's moving hand. "Maybe, but he won't understand."

"How about you try me?"

Tabitha eyed the dress. "Black?"

"Navy." Jackie added some silver to it and then turned the sketch for Tabitha to have a better view. "With shimmering stones. Knee length but fitted." She added the details to her list.

She nodded her agreement. "The book they're reading in class is *Little Women*."

Jackie searched the porcelain-skinned face for answers. "Why's that a problem? Can she not read? Maybe your dad can get her a tutor."

"She can read better than me. Charlotte's super smart. It's not about what she can do. It's that she doesn't want to because that was the book our mother read to us every night when we were younger and promised we'd always have each other. You know, grown-up lie stuff."

"But now she's gone."

"Right." Tabitha's voice dipped to a sad, brokenhearted tone.

Jackie studied the young girl and realized she didn't have a clue how to fix her life, not when she never even entered the coffee shop during toddler time. Kids were complicated and messy. Okay, these two weren't going to run around her shop and smudge handprints on her silk material, but they were still children. For some unknown reason, though, the sad little girl in the corner chiseled at her shield. Jackie went to the white chair and decided to try to involve Charlotte somehow. And if she knew anything about little girls, they all wanted to be princesses. "Hey, we're making a dress for your sister."

Charlotte nodded but kept her gaze on her moving feet. Flashes of the times she'd sat in the corner while her mother worked on her modeling when Jackie was always told to look pretty but keep her mouth shut flashed through her memories. It had been a lonely life where she'd never felt good enough to be Suzanne Raynor's daughter. "Would you like me to make you a dress, too? A princess dress?"

Charlotte shot up from the chair and ran to the table without a word, but she was communicating in her own way.

She ran back, grabbed Jackie's hand and heart, and dragged her to the table.

"Here," Jackie said. "Write out a list of everything you want on your dress—color, lace, design. Anything. Nothing is done well without a proper list." When Jackie sat down, the little girl with long blonde hair and big blue eyes crawled into her lap. To her shock, Jackie didn't think about how the girl was wrinkling her new capri pants or that she'd squished the bow. She only thought about how she wanted to make the most perfect dress that girl had ever worn, if only to see that bright smile again. After all, it wasn't like Jackie had to raise the rug rats. This was just make-believe, dress-up. They wouldn't be sticking around. There was no commitment to making a couple of dresses. It would be fun for a few days, and then she could concentrate on more important things. The wedding gowns, Knox Brevard's show, and her return to New York fashion life.

CHAPTER SIX

"Hey, Blaze. You have a visitor," Marco hollered from the firehouse living area.

Blaze put his mug of coffee down and headed out to find a tall, urban-type guy waiting for him. "What can I do for you?"

"I'm Knox Brevard from—"

"The internet show."

"You've seen it." The man smiled like a magazine cover model.

"No. I've heard about it around town since you've been running segments. I was at the Horton-Strickland wedding where you were filming the coffee segment, too."

"Right. You were there with Ms. Jacqueline Raynor, correct?"

Warning sirens blared in Blaze's ears. "No. I sat next to her because there was an open seat."

Knox moved closer, perhaps as if the men surrounding him were going to jump him if he said the wrong thing. "Can we speak somewhere more private perhaps?"

Rumblings from his fire brothers warned of a hazing later about this social call. "Here's good."

"Okay, well, the Knox Brevard show has reached international acclaim bringing business to Sugar Maple and reviving the town.

Some of our followers have deemed our show as The Match Maker. Now, I'm not taking credit for all the couples being joined through my show, but since this is the final segment, we thought it would be best to play into the audience's wishes."

"Oooh, Blaze is getting a woman," Marco shouted from the kitchen doorway behind Blaze.

He fisted his hands, not wanting to start an eruption of razzing for the rest of his shift. "Are you saying that you want to set me up with someone?"

"No, of course not. I'm not meant to find true love for you."

"That's good, because that nonsense doesn't exist." Blaze looked to his men to make sure they heard his words. "Not interested in love. I've got enough on my plate."

Knox stepped forward again, lowering his voice even a little more. "If there was a spark between you and Jackie, I'd like to know. The way you feel now would make the segment all the better. A divorcé with two young girls falls for a woman who hates children? Broken heart Blaze tames New York Fashionista's heart."

"Broken Heart Blaze. Hey, we've got a new nickname for Elijah."

"No," Blaze said in his deepest tone, making sure he was clear.

"I'm sorry. I didn't mean to overstep." Knox offered his hand. "I appreciate your time."

Blaze shook his hand, about-faced and marched into the kitchen, ending the impromptu meeting with some wanna-be actor with perfect hair and clothes. Blaze never trusted men who looked like they had their clothes tailor-made.

"It's your night to cook, Broken Heart Blaze," Marco said.

With a grunt, Blaze snagged a pan from the cabinet and slammed it down on the burner. "Dog food it is."

The men groaned and backed down, but he knew the comments would be rolling around the station for weeks if not months. Blaze wanted to give Knox Brevard a swift kick out of town and tell Jacqueline he was not on board with any of that show garbage. Besides, if Knox was right and Jacqueline really did hate kids, it didn't make a difference how beautiful or mesmerizing the woman was. He'd never give her the time of day. He'd finally managed to get his girls back. He wouldn't be involved with a woman who wouldn't welcome them into her life. No way, no how.

The dress would be made, he'd work on the cabinetry, and then they'd be done beyond the occasional running into each other at town events and coffee shops.

The evening rolled by like a rusted old bicycle with no wheels until a call came through. Blaze had never been so happy to have to fight a fire in his life. The adrenaline, fast pace, and siren blaring he lived for always distracted him from all his worries.

It wasn't until the next morning when his phone buzzed that he snapped back to reality. Ms. Miser had left him a voicemail requesting a meeting on Monday to discuss the options for Charlotte's reading issues.

Blaze rubbed his temple and slouched over the kitchen table.

"Rough night dreaming about the sexy Ms. Raynor, Broken Heart Blaze?"

He didn't bother to look up at Marco. Instead he washed the truck, sending the probie, Tom, inside to leave Blaze to his busy work.

To his disappointment, there were no more fires before his shift ended another twenty-four hours later. Twenty-four hours of teasing, tormenting, and torture about broken hearts and unattainable women. He'd held his tongue for twenty-three hours and twenty-two minutes until Marco handed him a Valentine's card allegedly signed by Jacqueline.

"Enough. I'm not some probie you can annoy every minute."

"Relax, we're just having some fun. Why you so worked up about this? We've teased you about women before. It's our way." Louis took a swig of morning coffee and then lowered it with a tight lip, teeth-showing smile. "Unless... Hey, men. He does like Jacqueline but knows he doesn't have a shot with her."

"I got a shot. I just don't want it." Blaze tossed his few remaining swallows of coffee down the drain and bolted to the bunks to retrieve his duffel.

Marco followed close behind. "No man, you don't. You're the kind of man that most women worship, but you don't score well with the uppity, ice queen types."

"She's not an ice queen. She's actually helping my oldest with a dress for the spring formal." He regretted oversharing before he even finished speaking.

"Spring formal?" Marco laughed. "Is that going to be your first date?"

"No, I'm not going to the formal. It's for my daughter's school. Speaking of, I need to get out of here to take care of some things before I go home."

"Like what?" Marco leaned against the wall. "Thought we were hanging today."

"Can't. I've got work this weekend."

"Work? Carpentry stuff? I'm in." Marco slung his own bag over his shoulder. "I need the money."

"Can't hire you." Blaze darted for the door in hopes he didn't have to explain further.

"Why not? I hired you for the last one. Thought we were a team for the contract work on our off days."

"We are, but this one doesn't pay."

Marco quirked a brow at him. "Then why you doing it?"

Blaze grabbed Marco and dragged him outside so no one else could hear. "Because it's a trade."

"A trade for what?"

Blaze eyed the area to make sure none of the other guys could overhear. "For the dress Jacqueline's making for Tabitha. It's the only way I could get her to agree, and right now, I need some major dad points with my girls. They still think I abandoned them, and no matter what I say, they won't think otherwise. The only way to win them over is to show them how much I care." Blaze waited for the teasing about Jacqueline, but it didn't happen.

Marco slapped him on the shoulder. "Listen. From one dad to another, stop trying to buy your girls' love. Just be there for them."

"I'm trying, but it's tough. I need to go buy that wood and make sure I'm not late this time to pick the girls up. I'll see you Wednesday."

Blaze decided he needed a mental health break before facing any more work or women so he hit the gym and then headed home to relieve the nanny. He imagined walking inside to open arms and smiles, but they didn't even look up from their plates of eggs and toast. "Let me shower, and then we can run out."

"We can stay here. I don't need a sitter."

He wasn't in the mood to battle with Tabitha, not right now. "Fine. I won't be gone long. I'm just running to take measurements for the cabinetry work I'll be doing at Ms. Raynor's store, and then I'll be home."

Tabitha and Charlotte exchanged a glance and then dropped their forks on their plates and raced to their rooms. "We'll be dressed in ten minutes. Wait for us!" Tabitha hollered.

He shook his head, not sure what had changed their minds. "Thanks for staying with them last night. I don't know what I'd do without you."

Whitney slinked between him and the refrigerator and ran her pointer finger down his cheek. "I don't mind. They're good kids." She smiled seductively. "You know, we haven't been out in a few months."

They'd broken up before she became the girls' nanny, and he thought they'd both be cool, but she'd become flirty again. He needed to keep the boundaries, or he'd have to look for a new nanny. That wouldn't be easy. He cleared his throat and stepped away. "I thought you were dating Ryan now."

She waved a long-nailed hand in front of her. "No, I only did that to make you jealous. How about tonight? We can go to town for some dinner or to my place?"

He fought for the right words that would keep her happy and watching his daughters since she was the best nanny in town and he wasn't going out with her again. There was a good reason he'd broken up with her a few months ago. He couldn't think of what it was now, but he knew there was one.

"Great, I'd love to go to dinner tonight." Tabitha held up a dress and then the other. "Which one do you think Ms. Raynor will like? I mean, you know her best, right?"

His little girl winked at him and then smiled at Whitney. He'd never been so happy to see his daughter butt in where she didn't belong.

"Now that I think about it, we can't go out with you tonight." She looked toward the ceiling with a faux searching expression. "Daddy will be way too busy helping Jackie, and we'll probably be staying well into dinner, if not well into the night. Maybe next time."

Whitney whirled around on him. "So the rumors are true? You and Jackie? One of the Fabulous Five who were my high school rivals?"

"It's not like that." Blaze attempted to calm Whitney.

"Oh, it's exactly like that." Tabitha turned and sauntered down the hallway, abandoning him to an extremely angry Whitney, who looked like she'd start throwing things at any moment.

CHAPTER SEVEN

Jackie finished rearranging the store so that Blaze could start working on her shelves and front store window boxes. It felt good to cross another item off her list. Time clicked away, and she worried that he'd renege on his deal. Would she finish the dresses for those two sweet girls anyway? How could she not?

Her frustration rose to the next level when lunchtime arrived and there was still no sign of him. When the door finally did open, Tabitha and Charlotte rushed in, looking like made-up dolls. Apparently their mother hadn't shown Tabitha how to wear makeup, and poor Charlotte's hair was a mess. Blaze followed in behind them wearing a too-tight T-shirt, jeans, and work boots. He could pull off the perfect sexy carpenter role for a movie.

Jackie sashayed out from behind the counter with all her attitude floating along with her striking green dress she'd chosen to wear today, knowing that a man would be coming into the shop. Not that she cared specifically about Blaze. Her mother had drilled it into her that a lady should never look less than her best when a man would be around. "Nice of you to show. I was about to lock up for lunch."

"I worked." He pulled out his tape measure, pencil, and pad and set to work near the front window.

She handed him the list of what she wanted for the shelves.

"What's this?" He only glanced over his shoulder but didn't take the paper.

She set it down on top of his toolbox. "It's a list of how I want this done."

"I don't have time for any changes. And I don't do lists."

She gasped at the idea and thought about interrogating him about how he ever got anything done but decided that would be too long of a conversation. "You got off before I even woke up today. What took you so long to get here?" Jackie tapped her platform white and green strappy heels.

"I didn't give you a time."

Tabitha eyed the new summer dresses Jackie needed to steam before hanging up. "It's not his fault. Whitney had a fit because he was coming to see you."

Jackie's hair rose at the name. They had been labeled arch enemies since they could pull each other's pig tails in preschool. "I see." She flattened an unruly poof at the edge of her skirt.

"Can I see the finished design?" Tabitha asked, standing up on her toes like a child trying to see candy in a store window. "Charlotte wants to see hers too."

"Sure. That way we can get your father's approval before I start working on it."

"Charlotte doesn't need a dress." He pulled out the tape measure and then scribbled something on his pad, not even noticing Charlotte's pout until she stomped her foot and crossed her arms over her chest. "What? You don't have a dance to go to."

"But a princess still needs a ball gown. Don't worry. It's on the house." Jacqueline retrieved a hairbrush from behind her counter and went to work on Charlotte's hair.

"I don't know why she'd need one, but that's fine." Blaze continued his measuring and recording and ignoring what was important.

Jackie turned over the Closed sign for lunch and then retrieved her sketchbook and waved the girls over to the glass table. They both shot to her side, Charlotte leaning into her with quick breaths and an intense smile. She tugged on Jackie's shirt and put her pointer finger to her chest like a woodpecker drilling a hole.

"Okay, you first."

Charlotte bounced in her chair, and Jacqueline savored her joy at seeing one of her designs. "We can change anything you want. This is all about you, Princess Charlotte." Jackie opened the sketchbook and flipped to Charlotte's Cinderella-inspired dress. Baby blue, ruffled neckline, with puffed chiffon sleeves but with a little bedazzle on the bodice and a sequin design of a pumpkin carriage down the front of the skirt.

Charlotte gasped and clapped.

The sound coming from his child must've drawn Blaze's attention, because he stood, dropped the tape measure to the floor, and strutted over. "Can I see?"

Charlotte snatched the sketchbook and turned it around to show her father.

"Wow, that's some dress." He offered a forced grin, but Charlotte didn't notice her father's lack of enthusiasm because she turned the pad around and hugged it to her chest, looked at Jackie, and mouthed, *Thank you.*

"Charlotte, you will be a princess for sure." Tabitha provided more of what Charlotte was looking for in a reaction. She shot her dad a sideways glower and then smiled at Charlotte. "I hope the dress Jackie designed for me is half as pretty as yours. Can I look at mine now?"

Obviously happy with her sister's words, Charlotte held out the sketchpad, and Jackie took it to flip to the next page.

"Perfect!" Tabitha exclaimed, drawing Blaze to look over their shoulders.

"No. Not happening. No way," Blaze said in an authoritative tone.

"You don't like my design?" Jackie said in a tone that told him he better backpedal his statement and quick.

"Dad doesn't know fashion. Don't listen to him," Tabitha said in a defiant tone.

"You will listen to me. I'm your father, and as your father, I'm telling you that no little girl of mine is going to wear that in public."

Tabitha shot off the chair like a Tasmanian devil on Red Bull. "You ruin everything. I hate you!"

Charlotte bolted to the chair, closed her eyes, and kicked her feet back and forth as if she were swinging. Blaze stood back with arms over his chest and his eyes narrowed. Tabitha stood with arms back, fisted hands, and a stare that could melt the Eiffel Tower on a winter's day.

"Would you excuse us for a minute, Tabitha?" Jackie tilted her head toward Charlotte. "Why don't you go calm your sister while I speak with your dad. Okay?"

Tabitha's pressed lips relaxed, her fingers unfurled, and she morphed into the sweet young lady Jackie knew she could be. "If you think that's best."

"I do." Jackie waited for Tabitha to cross the store and then stood to face an open-mouthed, wide-eyed Blaze.

"How'd you do that?"

"Do what?"

"Tame the teen out of her." Blaze blinked, his gaze still on his daughters as if he feared them.

"Sit," Jackie ordered.

He snapped back to the moment and lifted his chin. "My little girl is not wearing that grown-up dress."

"News flash... Tabitha isn't a little girl anymore, but if you want to stop having a constant war with her, you'll sit down and listen to me for a minute."

He scanned the room as if looking for another option, and when he didn't find one, he sat in the chair where Tabitha had been and clasped his hands in his lap. "I'll listen, but you won't change my mind. I'm her father, and I have a right to tell her no. Boys will get the wrong idea if they see her in that dress. You did this to me on purpose, didn't you?"

Jackie laughed. "Let me make this clear. I don't care enough about you to think about doing anything to you. I'm trying to help out your daughter."

"Only because she blackmailed you."

"Because I see a lot of me in her, and I want to help her."

Blaze shook his head. "It's worse than I thought."

"What is?"

"Raising Tabitha. She's a mystery to me. Like you. I know women—trust me, I do—but you and Tabitha are not like other women."

"I'll take that as a compliment. I can only imagine the women you know." She held up a hand before he stoked her combative attitude any further. The girls would be proud of her for how she'd controlled herself so far, and she planned on remaining calm. "As for the dress..."

"A dress you should know is too adult for her. I trusted you."

"The dress Tabitha wanted was black, strapless, with a skirt that barely covered her unmentionables."

"What?"

"She wants to be grown up, and you want her to be a little girl. This dress is for a teenager. You need to open your eyes and realize you can't treat her like a little girl or you'll lose her. At the same time, there must be reasonable boundaries. And I do mean reasonable. Not *alpha male, I'm in charge* kind of laws."

He eyed the dress on the paper. "That's appropriate for a young...teenager?"

"I assure you it is. Now, I think you should go purchase the wood and think about how you might better communicate with your daughter instead of barking at her. You left your girls when they were young, and their mother has abandoned them, so they don't trust any parental figure."

Blaze shot tall. "I didn't."

Jackie held up one hand. "Not what I think. What they think."

He eyed them, but his face was still tense. "Okay, I'll head out to get the wood, but they'll come with me. I need to talk to them. They're my responsibility."

"No. Now isn't the time. Do you see how Tabitha is sending you the NeoRent warning stare?"

"Ah, yeah. I know the one." He chuckled softly, but the pain in his face told her that the man struggled to connect with his daughters. If only her father would've tried that hard, maybe she would've had a happier childhood. Instead of having things, she could've had love. "That's why you both need space. Let me speak with her, and you can think about why you still see her as a little girl and what you can do to change the way you treat her, or I'm warning you she'll do something stupid to get away from you and find love somewhere else."

His jaw twitched, and Jackie knew she'd struck the *Daddy's little girl* protective chord. "That right there. That's what you need to dial down. Got me?"

He shook his head. "How do you know so much about kids?"

It was her turn to laugh. "I know nothing about raising children. I'd be an incredible failure at being a mother. What I do know is that teenage girls who are into fashion and noticing boys don't need a father who doesn't trust them enough to wear an age-appropriate dress. Now, you go. I've got the girls for a while."

"Why would you do that? You don't even like children."

"Because they're going to help me unpack the new spring lines and do some odd chores around here. They're going to help earn their dresses, too."

"And you think you can handle them for an hour?" He raised both brows at her.

"As good as your psycho ex-girlfriend, who I know is crazy." She stood and eyed the girls.

"I don't know about this. I'm not sure they want to stay with you. I don't want them to feel like I'm abandoning them again."

"Hey, girls... Who wants to help me unpack the new spring line and figure out how to set up a fashion display for the front window your father is building the platform for?"

"I do!" Tabitha shouted.

Charlotte bolted from the chair and pointed at her chest like the pesky woodpecker again.

"Or would you rather go get wood with me?" Blaze asked with such enthusiasm, Jackie felt bad for the man when they both looked at him like he'd grown a magical beard of stupidity.

CHAPTER EIGHT

Blaze pulled his truck in behind Jacqueline's shop and opened up the tailgate to the fresh smell of sawdust instead of the perfume and attitude he was about to experience inside that darn store. He might have taken a little longer than necessary to get the wood and the detour by his house to get his other tool bag. Served her right for thinking she knew his daughters better than he did. If he'd thought about it, he should've stopped for a sandwich on the way back just to give her more time to see she didn't know everything about everyone.

With a half smile and renewed energy, Blaze hopped out of the truck, spotting Knox and Stella approach from around the side of the building. "Hey man, you need help with that?"

Blaze looked at the man's dress clothes and shook his head. "Nah, I got it, but thanks." He eyed the two of them. "You just come from Jacqueline's shop?"

"Yep," Stella said with an air of *duh*.

He eyed the wheel of his truck to keep his amusement from showing to the others. "I guess it must be chaos in there."

"Why's that?" Stella asked, obviously trying to cover for her friend.

"You know, 'cause of my kids. It's not like Jacqueline Raynor knows how to handle children. I mean, my girls are sweet and all, but they're kids." Blaze forced a steady tone to his voice so Stella wouldn't catch on to his pleasure at Jacqueline's struggles.

Stella slid her hand into the crook of Knox's arm. "Women can surprise you."

Knox kissed her cheek. "They sure can."

Blaze averted his gaze to his work, sliding a board from the back of the truck and resting it on his shoulder. They had to be covering for her. When he entered the shop, he'd find a different story of what was going on with Jacqueline and the children.

"Your kids are darling. Any chance you'd let them model their new Raynor originals for the camera?" Knox asked.

Blaze adjusted his grip on the wood, catching a splinter in his thumb. He hissed and tried to yank it out, but some wood remained under his skin. Oh well. He'd deal with it when he got home. He'd been so distracted, he'd forgotten to put on his gloves.

"You all right over there?" Stella asked in an overly sugary, non-Stella tone.

"Fine," Blaze grunted.

"The girls modeling?" Knox asked again, as if Blaze had forgotten the question.

His first instinct had been to say no, but that hadn't worked well for him yet. Jacqueline's advice echoed in his head with caution. Darn woman was invading his mind now. "I don't know. I'll think about it."

"I know it would mean a lot to the girls and to Jackie," Stella said, enunciating Jackie as if she were the important person in that statement.

"As I said, I'll consider it." Blaze wanted to ask more about what was going on in the shop and what Stella meant by women can surprise you, but he thought better of it, afraid Knox might consider that an open door to him being in the segment dating

Jacqueline. The idea was still absurd, even if the kids hadn't destroyed her shop.

He made his way up the back stairs and knocked, but no one answered. They'd probably tied Jacqueline to a chair. He managed to wrench open the door and make his way inside to find the girls sitting at the table drawing with Jacqueline in between them. They looked cozy and happy. Why couldn't the girls look that happy when he was with them? He recalled a page from that parenting book he'd picked up about enjoying what your kids like to do instead of forcing them to like your activities. Maybe they were into drawing and he needed to try that, too. He could do stick figures and puppy faces. "I'm back."

The girls didn't even look up at him. "Yeah." Jacqueline pointed to the front window as if he'd forgotten why he was there. "Told you we'd be fine."

He tossed the wood onto the floor too hard but still didn't get much of a response from anyone. "What are you gals drawing? Maybe I could draw, too."

"We're not drawing," Tabitha said with a *geesh* chaser.

Charlotte looked up at him and shook her head and then held up her paper. She'd drawn a long pink skirt with some flowers on it.

"Dress, huh?"

"Yep, that's what I do here—sketch and make and buy and sell fashion. Your Tabitha has an eye for it by the way. As does Charlotte. They each have their own style. And they're both creative beyond their years."

Tabitha smiled like he'd never seen her smile since she'd arrived in Sugar Maple.

"Maybe I could get you some books on design or something."

"Books? Really? Is it 1988? That's what the internet's for—not to mention I have my own New York designer here to coach me."

"Ms. Raynor is far too busy to help two little girls with drawing clothes."

"Sketch. Fashion," Tabitha corrected, her smile fading quickly.

"Why don't you get to building while we finish up our sketches." Jacqueline nudged him out of the conversation, and he welcomed it. That's what he did all afternoon. They worked helping customers, bagging merchandise in fancy tissue paper and bags, and Charlotte would even greet people at the door with a smile but still no words. He almost felt bad for the girls being there all day on the weekend. Did Tabitha know he was doing this for her?

When Jacqueline turned the sign to Closed, he packed up his tools and eyed the girls, who were sorting and folding scarves in the back room, through the split in the white curtains. Jacqueline handed him a hammer and, to his shock, removed her shoes and sat on the floor near his work area. "You know, those two girls are pretty amazing."

"I'm glad you think so. They seem to feel the same way about you." Blaze had to admit it aloud, even though it hurt to face the fact that a stranger connected better with his girls than he did.

"They'll see how amazing you are soon, too." She patted his hand with such tenderness, he guessed she wanted something.

Blaze retreated and tossed the hammer into his tool bag before the warmth from her touch distracted him into agreeing to do something else. Since when did a woman control his thoughts and actions? Still, her words echoed in his head, bouncing around until a wayward thought exited his mouth. "You think I'm amazing?" He sounded like a prepubescent teen the way he said it. "I just mean, you think I have amazing traits my daughters will see?"

"No."

That one word from Jacqueline's lips deflated his mood. "I see."

"I don't think they'll see it. You'll have to show them. Nonetheless, I know you care about them and you have some good qualities, even if you're a little rough around the edges."

He dug his nail into the splinter in his finger so he didn't have to look at her. "Maybe you can help smooth some of those edges. For the girls, I mean."

"I can try." She leaned in and took his hand, studying his thumb with her soft green eyes. "I can get that out for you."

He tensed at her touch but then found how quickly he relaxed and settled into the contact. "I forgot... You're Jacqueline Raynor, fashionista. I'm sure you have tweezers here."

"I don't walk around plucking my eyebrows at work, but I am a seamstress, which means I have needles."

He yanked his hand away. "I'll get it out when I get home."

She leaned away, swiping her hair behind her shoulder and revealing a long, snow white neck. "Why, is Blaze Warren, fire-fighter extraordinaire, afraid of needles?"

"No, of course not. I was in med school years ago."

"Then what is it?"

He took in a stuttered breath. Blood, guts, snakes, bees, nothing scared him, but the sight of a needle sent shivers down his spine. With a quick glance to make sure the girls weren't in earshot, he cleared his throat. "Fine, I'm not afraid of them. I just don't like them."

He braced for Jacqueline's teasing, but it didn't come. Instead, she rose, went to the back room, and returned with a small needle.

"I promise it won't hurt."

"You can't tell any of the men about this—or my girls. I'd never live it down at the station."

"You can entrust me with your secret." She tucked her full auburn hair behind her ear and studied his thumb. "When did you realize you had a problem with needles?"

He studied the way her long lashes fluttered as she looked at his thumb so he wouldn't look at the needle. No way he'd pass out or vomit in front of her and the girls. "I don't know. It was around the time that Angela told me we were going to have a child. We were so young. I'd planned to marry her after college anyway, but we just sped up our timeline. We lost that first baby, but fourteen months after we were married, Tabitha was born. She was premature. The stress of me working and going to school was too much on Angela, and she went into early labor. When I saw my baby girl with needles stuck in her tiny frame, pumping things in and out of her body, I think I snapped. That's when I dropped out of med school and took a job in construction. I knew I didn't want to be an absentee father, and I couldn't be away from my baby girl as she struggled to breathe and eat. Ever since then, I haven't liked needles. I'm actually petrified of them."

"All done." Jacqueline pressed her lips to his thumb. It was brief but life altering. He'd never felt so cared for in his life. It was his job to care for everyone else, but in that moment, he forgot his man code and savored the touch of a beautiful and surprisingly caring Jacqueline Raynor.

"Thanks," he mumbled, "I better get the girls home. I'll be back tomorrow when their nanny gets there."

"No! We want to come back here tomorrow," Tabitha hollered from the back area, curtain pulled open. Charlotte stomped her foot and snarled like she belonged in a Stephen King movie where the sweetest person turns insane.

"Listen, it's best that you girls are at home and not in Ms. Raynor's way." Blaze retrieved his tool bag and stacked the remaining pieces of wood in the corner. "Let's go."

"That's a shame. I thought we'd all have a tea party tomorrow for lunch." And with that one sentence, it was as if Jacqueline had waved her magical parenting wand and the girls fell all over her.

"No," he blurted. But when the girls looked at him, he swore he'd turned into the wicked queen who had sent a dragon to eat a pumpkin carriage with Pinocchio inside of it.

CHAPTER NINE

The firm tone of Blaze's voice left no room for questioning his answer to her tea party suggestion. "Why?" Jacqueline cleared her throat. "I mean, they've been a big help today, and I could use more assistance tomorrow since I'll be boxing the fall collection to ship out."

Strange. She usually liked the quiet of her shop and the sophistication of it, but today she'd been happy. The kind of happiness she couldn't remember ever feeling before except in high school with her friends. The two young ladies with all their enthusiasm brought back the joy of designing. Something she hadn't felt in a long while. "Besides, I need to work on their dresses. I can't do that if I don't have my models."

"They're not models." Blaze grabbed his bag but halted at the edge of the front counter. "I mean, I didn't agree for them to do any modeling. I want them to be regular little girls without getting mixed up in all this internet show madness."

"I only meant—"

His tense, protective father face appeared. "I know you want your shop to receive worldwide recognition from the internet show, but I don't want my girls used as a pawn in this situation."

"I assure you, Mr. Warren. I would never do such a thing. Even I have boundaries. I only meant that they needed to come for an initial fitting. I'd planned on working on their dresses this evening, so tomorrow would work perfectly for them to come back and try them on, but if you'd rather leave them at home with your ex and you believe that's the better choice, then so be it." Jackie waved the girls to their father. "If you change your mind, I'll be here tomorrow at ten until two. If you think you can make it between those hours, that would be good."

Tabitha paused a foot away from him and snarled, "You always ruin everything." She took Charlotte by the arm and marched out the back door.

Jackie turned away so he couldn't see the glint of disappointment moistening the corner of her eyes. Anger and resentment welled up inside her. The fact that the man actually believed her to be so cold and heartless hurt more than it should. Not to mention that these two little dresses she'd designed brought more excitement than anything else she'd worked on in the last year. Maybe this would awaken her muse, which had been hibernating the last twelve months.

"Jacqueline. I…I didn't mean to offend you." His tone softened to apologetic. "It's just that I didn't think you'd want them here."

"You should go. I need to keep up my end of the bargain and get the girls' dresses started. Be here tomorrow before two. That's if your nanny shows up on time." Jackie shot through the curtains to her back room and waited for the click of the door. She peered out the window to see Tabitha and Charlotte with their backs toward their father, letting him know how they felt. They were right. The man was a NeoRent. Just like her own father, he didn't understand that little girls needed their dad's love, not judgment and avoidance.

When the truck pulled out of the back lot, she didn't want to head home for her usual glass of red wine, hot bath, and quiet time. She wanted to work. The two little girls had inspired her, and work she did. Designing and putting together the bodice and skirts of both dresses, she worked until well into the early morning hours and must've fallen asleep at some point. She awoke with chiffon blue material stuck to her face and a kink in her neck.

She closed up, turned out the lights, and headed home but couldn't sleep. The ideas were poring through her. Nothing she could actually take to New York or share on Knox's show, but she sketched them anyway. By six in the morning, she'd napped twice and created new summer dresses, jumpers, and tops for teens and young girls. They were perfect for the younger frame, innocent but with a grown-up flare. She eyed the designs and decided she could make them for Charlotte and Tabitha if they wanted them. That was if NeoRent would allow it.

She took an hour to get dressed and wished the girls would be coming over for a fitting so she could see how her designs looked on them, but either way she'd return to the store to work on fabric and fringe choices for the new outfits.

At eight she made her way to meet her friends at church, and then they headed to Maple Grounds for a bit. Sunday was their no-guy time for just the girls. She treasured this one hour a week they'd meet without their boyfriends after church, no excuses. This allowed her to enjoy her visit with them without being forced to watch all her friends going googly eyed over their boyfriends and fiancés.

Jackie was energized with new ideas and ready to head to work, but her eyes were getting sticky from lack of sleep.

"What's got you so distracted today?" Stella asked.

Jackie tried to give her best innocent look. "What do you mean?"

Felicia jumped in, obviously wanting to make sure Stella didn't overstep. "You're quiet today. You haven't, well, made any snide remarks to Stella or judgmental looks at Carissa's clothes."

Jackie tried to remain neutral in her expression, not wanting to tell the girls too much about her new inspiration. "No reason to, I guess."

"Ah, you did see that I'm wearing Keds to church, right? I mean, it wasn't my fault. Roxy stole one of my sandals and hid it. Who knew cats could be so mischievous?"

"They don't look bad. It's spring." Jacqueline eyed the shoes and found them nondescript enough not to matter.

"You're the one who said anything with a rubber sole is a sin on Sunday." Mary-Beth set a welcomed mug in front of Jacqueline.

The smell of the eye-opening espresso drew her in quick, and the warm, milky flavor went down smooth. "Oh, that's good. Thanks."

"You just drank something without complaining that you don't need the calories. Okay, what happened? Did you put your stilettos on the wrong feet?" Stella moved in an inch from Jackie's face.

"Down, girl. I thought Knox had housebroken you." Jackie coveted her warm, perfectly brewed beverage.

"There she is." Stella laughed and sat back in her seat. "Now what's up?"

Jackie forced an innocent smile. "Nothing. You're the one Knox nicknamed Stiletto Stella."

"You knew about that?" Stella's eyes darted about the room, but apparently no one cared about invading her life because they all kept their eyes on Jackie. She usually liked all eyes on her when she was in a room, but not today.

"Maybe we're asking the wrong question. Who's up?" Carissa asked with that not-so-innocent smile of hers.

Jackie shook her head, still keeping a plain expression. "Nothing. I just didn't get much sleep last night."

"Oh, do tell." Mary-Beth sat down before she'd finished delivering coffee to everyone. No one seemed to care, though. All their attention was on Jackie.

"Because I was sketching." She huffed, still trying not to give too much ammo her friends could overanalyze and shoot back at her later.

"Why were you doing that? I thought you'd already done all the fashion week knock-offs," Stella announced to the world.

"They aren't knock-offs. They're designs that I've tweaked to meet the needs of this town. This is the thanks I get for trying to bring some fashion to Sugar Maple?"

"Knock-offs." Stella darted to retrieve the other mugs Mary-Beth had abandoned on the counter before Jackie could respond.

Jackie took another sip, savoring the way it provided a moment of bliss before she answered. "I'm not working on the spring and summer lines anymore. Besides, these are complete originals." She bit her tongue, but it was too late. The information had already slid out of her mouth and into the ears of her interfering and obnoxiously caring friends.

"What? You're sketching your own stuff again? Stuff you weren't asked to do, not any tweaks of other designs? Honest to goodness, your own designs you've been inspired to create? That's amazing." Felicia sat forward expectantly. "This is huge. You said you hadn't come up with anything since you'd arrived home. That the town sucked the creativity out of you. Oh no... Does this mean you'll abandon us again for New York? I mean, I'd be happy for you but sad all at the same time."

"Relax. These designs aren't New York fashion. They're for teenage girls. I made them for Tabitha and Charlotte."

Carissa tilted her head. "You mean Blaze's girls?"

Stella clapped her hands together once. "I told Knox you had the hots for the fireman. He said no way you'd stoop to date a civil servant."

"I'm not dating anyone." For some reason, Jackie didn't like the way Stella put Blaze down, as if serving the people in their community wasn't a good thing. She wasn't about to defend him right now, though. Not when he thought so little of her, and not when her friends were looking for a reason to overanalyze her nonexistent dating life. "Besides, the man thinks I'm a bad influence on his kids. He accused me of using them so they'd help me look good on the Knox Brevard show." She shot a look around the table, waiting for someone to agree with him, but none of her friends looked anything but shocked at the accusation.

"You wouldn't do that. You might steal someone's designs, or burn their fashion line, but you'd never harm a child," Stella said, and the rest nodded in agreement.

Jackie would argue, but back in the day, she'd done both to sabotage other designers' work, as did everyone else in New York to get ahead. Not set fire to someone's line because someone could get hurt, but sabotage with paint or a seam ripper perhaps. It was a cut or be cut kind of business. She'd once missed the competitiveness and action of the fashion world, but at the moment, it didn't sound enjoyable at all. She was getting too soft and needed to start working toward the goal of returning to New York before she found herself stuck in Sugar Maple the rest of her life. It was good for her friends but never the plan for Jackie herself. She was supposed to be a star like her mother.

Felicia nudged closer to the table. "I think Blaze Warren is amazing. Do you know he's the one who organizes the toy drive every Christmas for the fire department?"

"Probably feels guilty for losing full custody of his children when they were young," Jackie shot back.

Mary-Beth shook her head. "No. According to Ms. Horton…I mean Mrs. Strickland—geesh, I need to get used to her married name. Anyway, according to her, Blaze fought for his marriage and for his kids, but in the end he accepted visitation to stop the fighting that was harming his girls. The ex-wife wouldn't back down and had created a horrible situation for all of them. He stopped fighting so the girls could live in peace."

Jackie ran her finger around the rim of her mug "I didn't know. I mean, he mumbled something about his past, but I wasn't listening." She straightened in her chair, all of a sudden wanting to return to her shop to speak with Blaze again. Apparently there was more to his story than she'd thought originally. She pushed the cup to the center of the table and stood.

"Where are you going?" Mary-Beth asked.

"Work. I'm inspired to sketch again. Perhaps my muse will give me something I can use for New York. Besides, I have two wedding dresses to work on." She nudged Stella, who grimaced. "I've ordered lace from Paris."

Stella shot up, and Jackie waited for her onslaught of insults and snide remarks, but instead she collapsed back into her seat. "That's great."

"It is?" Jackie asked before she thought better of it.

Stella picked up her cup and held it up as if to toast. "Sure. It'll be perfect for your wedding to Elijah 'Blaze' Warren."

CHAPTER TEN

Tabitha and Charlotte sat at the kitchen table with his coffee already made and waiting for him when he returned from the hardware store. "Ah, what's going on? We already ate breakfast."

"This isn't breakfast. It's a father intervention," Tabitha said with Charlotte nodding beside her.

Blaze eyed the escape route, but despite the fact they were obviously unhappy with him, the good news he saw in this was that they actually wanted to have a conversation with him. Well, Tabitha did, Charlotte would only grunt, use her hands and feet, or nod and shake her head. Still, it was progress from the cold silent treatment he'd received last night. "Okay, I'm listening."

"Sit down, please." Tabitha scooted the chair out with her foot and then sat straight and folded her arms, resting her elbows on the table. Charlotte copied her big sister.

He removed his jacket and draped it over the back of the chair, readying himself for their complaints about his NeoRent treatment. "Okay, I'm listening." He didn't want to be rude since they'd taken the trouble to make him coffee, so he took a sip. He concentrated on not making a face at the bitter flavor.

"We think you should ask Ms. Raynor out on a date."

He spewed coffee all over the table.

"Ewww, Dad!" Tabitha wiped her forehead, and Charlotte grabbed a dishtowel for him.

"Sorry." He coughed out the liquid that had made it up his nose. "Um, I don't understand. I thought you were going to give me a hard time about the nanny coming over."

Tabitha took the dish towel from Charlotte and tossed it to his chest. "That's not an issue. It's been taken care of."

"What do you mean?" he asked, not sure he wanted to know the answer.

Both girls eyed each other, obviously in cahoots. Tabitha cleared her throat. "Listen, you're not getting any younger, and Ms. Raynor is a beautiful and talented woman. You'd be lucky to go out with her. She's a step up from your normal choices."

"You do realize I dated your mother, right?"

Charlotte shot a look at Tabitha, as if his point had merit, but apparently Tabitha decided to ignore him. "We've decided that if we're going to live with you and you'll eventually have a woman in your life, we should have a say in who that woman is since it affects us, too."

He rolled through his parental conversations with the men at his firehouse, his ex-wife before she'd sent the girls to him, and Jacqueline. None of it gave him information on what to do in this situation. "Listen, I'm not going to get married, so you don't have to worry about it." He eyed them both and saw the concern on their faces. More than anything, he didn't want them to worry. He wanted to make his girls happy and make them feel loved and secure.

"You will. Men have to have women in their lives."

"But I have you two now. That's enough women in my life," he teased, but they didn't look amused.

"You'll date, and if we don't want to be shipped off again, we want to be friends with who you go out with. We didn't like

Mom's boyfriend and let him know it, so we got shipped away." Tabitha lifted her chin in obvious defiance. "We're done being shipped away."

"Oh honey, I won't do that. I told you, I've fought to have you in my life for years. From the day your mother and I broke up, I wanted you in my life."

"But we weren't." Tabitha stated the fact, but he knew she didn't understand the reason it happened that way.

"I know, but...well, it was complicated." He tried to think of a way to explain it without making their mother a villain. That wasn't the answer to any of this. No matter how he felt about his ex, he'd never poison his children against her.

Charlotte looked up with big expectant eyes, drawing his heart to her.

"Listen, girls. You know you did nothing wrong in any of the grown-up garbage that has been in your life. It isn't that your mother didn't want you. It's that it was my turn. She's had you all these years, and I wanted my opportunity. I admit, I pictured you returning to me as my baby girls, not all grown-up like you are."

"I'm not a baby," Tabitha said, but Charlotte was the one with an angry glare.

"I know that now. Before you arrived, I had an image of building you doll houses and braiding your hair."

"You know how to braid hair?" Tabitha asked with a hint of admiration in her voice.

"YouTube. I watched some videos before you arrived."

"You did that for us?" Tabitha's small mouth hung open.

"Of course. That's what I'm trying to say. I'm trying to be a good father, even if I fail a lot. But you two are such amazing young ladies. Together we can figure this out."

Tabitha reached across the table and took his hand, sending a zap of hope through him. "You're doing better."

Charlotte joined the family hand pyramid, laying her tiny fingers on top of theirs.

"I'll keep trying, too. I'm not going to lie. I love you both and my first instinct as a father is to protect you, but I'm learning that I have to be both mother and father to you. This is an adjustment for me."

"But if you marry Ms. Raynor, you wouldn't need to be."

"Whoooa, marriage? Nope. Not happening." He retreated from the table and their insane ideas. "Even if I wanted to remarry, I'd never marry Jacqueline. She doesn't even like kids, and you two are the most important people in my life."

"She does like kids. Well, she likes us. She said so."

"Even if she did, we're too different. She's high fashion. I'm high adrenaline. Hunting, fishing, and fighting fires I know. Fabric, lace, and shoes are not my thing."

"But that's what makes a woman a good mother and a man a good father. You're supposed to be different. Besides, Natalie Grenich says that opposites attract."

"Natalie who?" he asked.

"A girl from my class. She's dating a senior, so she understands these things," Tabitha said with all the innocence of a child.

He made a mental note to keep his daughter away from the worldly Natalie but didn't dare say it aloud, considering the progress he'd made with the girls.

Tabitha scooted her chair out. She walked around the table and placed one hand on his shoulder. "Don't worry, Dad. We've got this. We know what's best for you."

Charlotte joined her and placed her hand next to Tabitha's with a nod. They both left the room, and he knew he needed to do something to make them understand why this was an insane idea. "Wait, where are you going? We need to discuss this more."

"No time." Tabitha waved a hand above her head. "We have to get ready to head to the shop."

Blaze was done allowing them to think they were in control.

He was the father, and what he said stood. "You're not going. Whitney will be here any minute."

"No she won't. She canceled."

"What? Why?" He eyed his cell, but there were no missed calls. "She didn't tell me that."

"I don't think she'll call you again. She's been taken care of." The way Tabitha's voice sounded light but with an evil inflection made Blaze squirm.

"What do you mean, taken care of?"

They raced to their bedroom doors, and Tabitha hollered back, "We told her we didn't need her today since were going to the shop to plan the wedding. She said we'd have to find a new sitter for now on."

"Wedding? What wedding? I thought you were raised better than to lie to someone. I'm not marrying Jacqueline."

"We were talking about Stella's and Carissa's, but I'm glad you're starting to warm to the idea of marrying Ms. Raynor." Tabitha shut the door before he could open his mouth to argue.

How did he lose control so quickly? Boys would be so much easier. You tell them what to do and they do it. If he raised his voice at a little girl, she'd cry. Motherhood was tougher than he'd thought it could be.

He thought about calling Whitney to make a stand, but that would be too messy. They'd had a superficial relationship for years, and then it had turned...serious. Too serious. He didn't want serious. He'd tried that, and it was an epic fail. Except for his two daughters.

Before he could think of another battle plan to deal with the situation, the girls bounded out of their rooms and out the front door.

"Come on. You don't want to be late. I texted Ms. Raynor, and she said we'd have a tea party this afternoon while you worked. With real china and scones from Sugar and Soul Bakery. How amazing is that?"

He grabbed his keys, followed the girls like a lost puppy to the truck, and drove them to the shop while they rambled on about how excited they were to have their first ever afternoon tea. That's when he realized Charlotte had on her white gloves. He couldn't help but snicker at the idea that she'd dressed up as if she were going to see the Queen of Narnia.

"You girls look pretty," he said with real pride.

"Thanks." Tabitha adjusted her belt and put lipstick on that made her look like a working girl, but he held his words until he could think of the right way to approach the subject.

In that moment, he decided that arguing would get him nowhere, and if Jacqueline didn't mind the girls in the shop, it was better they were with him than with an ex-girlfriend-nanny. Not only because that sounded complicated, but he thought he was starting to understand the girls better. Perhaps even learning how to communicate with them a little more.

He drove past the store, noticing the Closed sign on the front door and wondered if she was there, but when he parked in the back, she opened the door and waved to them.

She stood on the back steps looking stunning in her sundress with see-through sleeves. When she turned, the buttons up the back reminded him of an old-fashioned ball gown. Had she designed that dress herself? If she had, it fit her perfectly. If he knew anything about fashion, he'd think she was talented, but his idea of fashion was not wearing plaid with stripes. Something he learned from his college girlfriend.

Maybe he *was* more Neanderthal than father. He raced around the truck and offered Tabitha his hand. "A gentleman should always open the door for you."

She giggled, took his hand, and smoothed out her top once she stepped aside, the way he'd seen Jacqueline smooth a skirt when she stood. Charlotte copied with a heart-thumping giggle, the first sound he'd heard out of her this morning, and it was magnificent. She held out her gloved hand, but he took her by the waist and twirled her once before setting her down. "And you, princess, are ready for the afternoon tea."

Her bun on top of her head fell to the side as if not secured with enough pins, but he didn't dare say anything. Tabitha took her by the hand and led her to an awaiting Jacqueline. "Are we dressed okay for afternoon tea?"

Jacqueline offered a smile that warmed the cool spring afternoon. "Perfect. Now, you may go sit at the table and put your napkins in your lap. I'll be there in a minute to pour the tea."

"Yes, ma'am." Tabitha opened the door and let Charlotte through ahead of her.

Once they were out of sight, Jacqueline came down and joined him at the tuck. "I'm glad you brought them today."

She sounded sincere, happy.

"I have to confess, there wasn't much of a choice."

"Oh." Jacqueline straightened the collar of his shirt, distracting him for a moment. "That's right. I heard the girls told Whitney you were going to be with me so she quit on you. Sorry about that."

"I'm not," he said before he thought better of it.

She looked up with a tilt of her head.

"I mean, since she can't work right now, they have to stay with me. It kind of works out since I want to spend more time with my girls, and what better way to do it than where they seem to be most happy."

She nodded and took a step back from him. "I'm going to go sit with the girls. There's a place set for you if you'd like to join us."

The idea of sitting with his girls and Jacqueline for any reason sounded great. "I need to get the window box done, though. Not to mention that I have to figure out how to find a nanny by the time I return to work on Wednesday, and Monday I have a meeting with the school about Charlotte."

"What about?" She led him up the stairs but paused at the

back door. "You don't have to share if you don't want to. I know it isn't my business."

"No, it's fine. It's just that they want her to leave Sugar Maple Elementary School because they stated they're not equipped to handle a child who refuses to speak."

"That's ridiculous. And you mean *Ms. Miser* can't handle it." Jacqueline frowned. Even without a smile, she was the most stunning woman he'd ever seen. The way the light cast golden highlights in her auburn hair made her look even more angelic. But he knew better. Jacqueline had as much venom as sugar in her blood.

He jumped ahead of her and opened the back door. "After you, my lady. Your royal subjects await."

She laughed, lifting the mood before they saw the girls.

"Look, Daddy. There's a place for you, too."

He stopped and eyed Charlotte, with the biggest smile on her face, tapping the seat at her side and knew he didn't stand a chance to say no. "Will you allow me at your table? All of you look so beautiful, and I'm in work clothes."

"Did you hear that? He called us all beautiful." Tabitha blinked, but Blaze was sure she'd meant to wink at Jacqueline.

"I'm sure we can make an exception this once," Jacqueline said.

Blaze pulled out Jacqueline's chair. "My lady."

The girls snickered, and he went to sit in the chair between them, but Tabitha hopped up and took it, leaving the one next to Jacqueline open. For once he knew what his daughter wanted, and he'd have to break her little heart later when he told her the truth that there was no way a beautiful, sophisticated woman like Jacqueline would ever settle for a man like him. She belonged in New York. He belonged in Sugar Maple. She hated children. He loved his girls. It would never work. Even if she did agree to go out with him, it wouldn't last. Just like his first marriage... A relationship with Jacqueline was doomed to fail.

CHAPTER ELEVEN

Jackie found her gaze traveling from the material she was pinning to fit the dress to Tabitha to a tight T-shirted Blaze. Why'd he have to take off his button-up? She'd known he was fit, but oh goodness, his muscles rippled with each move he made, and considering he was staining the platform he'd constructed, the movement was constant.

"Ouch." Tabitha jumped away.

Jackie realized she'd placed the pin too deep. "I'm so sorry. Are you okay?"

"Yeah." She rubbed her hip but looked to her father and then back to her. "I think it was worth it."

Busted.

Jackie forced her attention onto her work and far from the distracting Blaze and his muscles. "What do you think so far?"

"You still need to hem it, right? I mean, I don't want to look like a teacher."

"You also don't want to look like a working girl," Blaze called out, confirming he'd been paying attention to them even while he worked.

Tabitha spun. "Why not? Just 'cause I'm a woman doesn't mean I can't work."

"That's not what I meant. Never mind."

"I know what you meant. Not nice calling your daughter a—"

"Turn around and face me before I poke you again." Jackie watched Charlotte's attention narrow in on the conversation and decided this wasn't appropriate for a fourth-grade girl. Not that Jackie knew what was appropriate at what age. She was never around children, not even when she *was* a child. Except for the Fabulous Five, who she saw at school and during special meetings, she had lived in the adult world, modeling by the age of eight. Not that she minded. Playing dress-up always made her happy, and modeling jobs meant she'd make her mother happy.

She finished up with Tabitha's dress, pulling the hem an inch above the knee, feeling Blaze's scrutiny the entire time.

"No higher than that," he barked.

"It's an appropriate length for Tabitha's age. I might not know children, but I know fashion."

"You know about children." Tabitha kept her chin high and stood straight, probably to make sure she didn't get stuck by a pin again. "Charlotte says you're great with her."

"Charlotte told you that?" Jackie asked, feeling a little more important in the world.

"She did. And I agree." Tabitha wrapped her arms around Jacqueline, and Charlotte joined in. "Thank you for being our substitute mother."

Jackie choked at their words. The insanity of the notion she'd ever be a mother almost made her laugh aloud, but she didn't want to offend the girls. "Okay, go take those dresses off before you wrinkle them."

They shot to the dressing room, giggles penetrating the quiet of the room in pleasant harmony.

"I don't know why everyone thinks you're bad with kids. You're better than I am with them, and I'm their father." The way

Blaze looked to the ground when he spoke tugged at her in a way she hadn't expected. He looked vulnerable, unsure of himself. Normally the man strutted around like a Fire God.

"You're doing a great job with the girls. You're just going through an adjustment period, but you're giving them what they need, even if they aren't seeing it yet."

"What am I giving them?" he asked with both brows lifted high.

"Your time. Trust me, all a daughter wants is her father's attention. Once they have that, nothing else in the world matters. You make them feel important in your life, and they will have everything they need."

"They're important to me." He took in a deep breath and let it out slowly. "I thought they ditched the nanny so they could come spend time here with you."

She rubbed his arm. "They don't care about me. They're here to be with you but will probably never admit it to you."

"How do you know that?" Blaze asked with such eagerness.

"Because I would've done anything to win my father's attention." Jackie slid away before he knew how broken she truly was. No man liked a woman who was less than perfect.

He followed her to her office. "I'm sorry your father wasn't there for you."

"It's no big deal." She waved dismissively, but he stayed anyway.

His hand touched her shoulder, squeezing it in comfort like a friend. "It is a big deal. How could a father ever want anything more than his daughters?"

A lump the size of a bolt of fabric lodged in her throat. She couldn't speak, so she only shrugged. Not ladylike, but neither was crying.

"There isn't a man in this world who wouldn't want to be around you."

She turned with a forced grin she hoped didn't make her look like a possessed Grinch. “Of course men love a beautiful girl on their arm.”

“Don’t do that,” he said sternly.

“Do what?” She still clung to a light, uplifting spirited conversation.

He crossed the room and leaned his back against the far wall and looked at her, not in the way of a man checking out a pretty woman with a figure. More of a deep, analyzing, I-see-through-your-façade kind of gaze. “Yes, you’re physically gorgeous. I think you know that. But that’s not what makes you beautiful. Not to me anyway.”

Don’t go there. Don’t ask him, Jackie told herself, but curiosity took hold. “What makes me beautiful to you?”

He stepped forward, closing the space between them. Jackie’s pulse revved faster than her Brother sewing machine on hyper-speed. “There are so many things, but you won’t let me see them all. You pretend to be cold, but you’re kind.”

“I’m not kind. I’m selfish,” she shot back.

“That’s what you portray, not who you are. You hide behind it to protect yourself. Not sure from what, but perhaps it has to do with past relationships.”

“I think you’ve inhaled too much smoke during your firefighting.” She wanted to flee from the conversation yet was drawn to stay.

“You only prove what I’m saying. No woman would spend the time you have with my girls if she didn’t have a kind heart.” He closed the last few steps between them, stealing her air. “And you don’t hate children. You only say that.”

“I do. It’s just that Tabitha and Charlotte are unique. They make it easy to like them.” Jackie didn’t run from saying her feelings aloud, but it was easy when it came to those two girls.

He reached for her, but she pulled away. “You’re talented, brave, smart, and funny. Even when you don’t mean to be. And more than anything, my girls love you.”

"Love? Don't be ridiculous. They just care about my fashion and clothes." That one word made Jackie want to run. She escaped the small space and fled out to the main room in hopes the girls were there, but they weren't. They were still giggling in the changing room.

"Do you think you're so unlovable, Jacqueline Raynor?" he asked.

Her breath caught. No one had ever challenged her in such a way. She should turn around and tell him to leave, that he was wrong about her and that he needed to finish his job and get out of her life. And she would have too, but her phone rang. She darted to answer it. "Hey, Carissa. What's going on?"

"I'm afraid the spring formal is off," she said, her voice echoing from the speaker.

The words stunned Jackie. "No, that can't be true."

"It is. Apparently there was a mismanagement of funds by the PTA, and they're under investigation. Long story into a short reason, there are no funds for the dance."

Jackie looked to Blaze as if he held all the answers to the questions she'd never thought to ask. "Can we raise funds and donate it to the PTA?"

"No, not while they're being investigated."

"But they can't cancel the spring formal. It's a tradition," Jackie said, as if her saying so made it true.

"They're canceling the dance?" Tabitha's words sounded wounded and hollow.

Jackie turned around. She couldn't stomach seeing the child have her hopes and dreams shattered because of some crime. In that moment, for the first time in her life that she could ever remember, she didn't think about how this might affect herself. She thought about how it affected the young girl in front of her. Could Blaze be right? Could she really have a heart in her icy chest?

CHAPTER TWELVE

Blaze worked for hours, but his mind was on the way Tabitha had looked deflated since being told about the dance. He wanted to do something, anything, to be a hero to his daughter so that he could finally win her over. But how could he fix a school dance? When he finished painting, he stepped back and analyzed a job well done. But at the heavy sigh from the corner, he faced his girls, unable to take it any longer. And based on Jacqueline's moping, she had to be as disappointed as Tabitha was. "There has to be something we can do."

"I'll call a Fabulous Five intervention tomorrow, but I'll need a strategy. I can't expect the five of us to do everything."

Charlotte tapped him on the stomach to get his attention. She didn't speak, but she pointed at each of them standing in the room and Tabitha at her chair sulking.

"Of course we'll all help too, but there's so much that will have to be done. I honestly am not sure what all that is." Blaze admitted he hadn't been to a school dance even when he was in school.

"I am," Jacqueline said in a distant voice with a far-off gaze.

Tabitha stepped forward. "I've never been to a high school

dance, but I've seen them on movies. It has to be the same. We'll need things like balloons, decorations, food…what else?"

Charlotte ran to the register, pulled a piece of paper from the printer, and then returned, sat down at the table, and wrote the items already mentioned with perfect penmanship. She added beverages and entertainment to the list.

Had Charlotte always made lists, or was she mimicking Jacqueline? The girls had mentioned to him that she had a list for everything.

Jackie sat by her side, stroking Charlotte's blonde hair like a mother. "I didn't know how to spell some of those words until high school myself. You're a smart girl."

"I still don't know how to spell them," Blaze joked.

They all gathered around the table and finished a list they thought would be comprehensive enough.

"Don't worry. We'll figure this out," Blaze tried to reassure Tabitha, and Charlotte nodded vigorously. He eyed the fancy clock on the fireplace mantel that had flowers instead of logs in the hearth. "We should go. I need to get you girls fed, and I need to figure out a nanny for Wednesday night. That doesn't give me much time."

"I'll ask around for you," Jackie offered.

"Thanks. I better get the girls home before it gets too late."

"Aww," Tabitha cried out.

Charlotte stomped her foot.

"No, girls, it's a school night." Blaze tried to sound stern, but it was difficult with their pouty lips.

"You heard your father, and if you want me to finish your dresses, I need to get to work."

Blaze didn't really want to leave the shop. He felt safe with Jacqueline. The girls didn't treat him like he was fungus when she was around. "Thanks again for everything you've done."

"I make dresses. That's what I do." She shooed the girls to the back door, despite their moaning and big-lip-puppy-dog-eyes expressions.

The girls went to the truck, but he stalled an extra moment. "You've done more than that. The girls have really enjoyed their time here. It's nice to see them smile."

She tucked her hair behind her ear and licked her lips, drawing his attention to her perfect face. "Good night."

"Right, um, good night." Blaze darted down the steps, remembering his daughters and the fact that he looked like a NeoRent towering over Jacqueline in the doorway, stalling his exit. Why was life easier when she was around? Life had never been easy with Angela. She'd been complicated and upset all the time, and it was work to even be in the same house with her. He'd say it had fallen apart after her postpartum breakdown after Charlotte was born, but it was before that. From the moment they met, she'd been insecure and demanding and upset. By the time they finally divorced, he'd been exhausted.

"Dad, are you coming or are you going to stare at Jacqueline all night?"

Giggles drew him to his truck, where he tucked them safely inside and drove them home.

All night he tossed and turned, thinking about his failed marriage and how he knew he'd never put himself through that again. Freedom was easy. Relationships were tough. Besides, he was good at *getting* a woman. It was keeping her happy that was the struggle. A mind-numbing, miserable, heart-wrenching, nightmare of a life.

By morning, he was tired and thankful he could probably sneak a nap in later. Unfortunately, he first had to face Ms. Miser and the principle about Charlotte. He dropped Tabitha off at school first and then made his way to the elementary parking lot, where he parked and looked at Charlotte. "Honey, I love you. You're an amazing, smart, pretty young lady. You know that, right?"

She shrugged but didn't speak.

"Listen, I know you've been through more than a girl your age should have to go through. I wish I could've made your mother happy, but I never did. I wish I could've taken you with me after the divorce, but I made some mistakes that kept us apart. I wish I could've raised you myself, but I can't change any of that. All I can do is promise to do better for you. I'm here for anything you need, and I'm not going anywhere."

She smiled up at him, those big blue eyes like unicorn and puppy dog superglue stickers to his heart.

"I need you to try, too. Do you think you could speak for me? The counselor said that I should be patient, and I am, but this isn't about me. The school says you have to speak if you want to stay in class."

She opened her mouth, but only air came out, no sound. Big tears welled in her eyes, and he wanted to march into that school and pummel someone until they understood that his daughter had a right to be at school like any other child. That they should figure out how to accommodate her needs. But he wouldn't. He was a father now, and his fighting days were over. He pulled her to his chest and hugged her tight. "Don't worry. We'll figure something out."

They entered the school, and Charlotte slid her hand into his, making him feel like he wanted to dance or sing through the hallway. It was the first time she'd initiated any contact with him since she'd arrived, excluding with Tabitha and Jacqueline also in the mix. In that moment, he felt like a real dad.

"Mr. Warren. Charlotte." A woman with a starched button-up top, straight skirt, and overdone makeup led them into the principal's office, where Ms. Miser already sat waiting. He couldn't help but see a lion ready to pounce, with her wild orange hair with matching lips and tarantula eyelashes.

"Please have a seat and we'll get started." The principal

pointed to the only remaining chair, so Blaze sat and put Charlotte on his lap.

"We called you here today to discuss Charlotte's class participation," Principal Young said in a friendly, calm tone. "I understand Charlotte hasn't spoken in some time. Although technically we can accommodate her, we feel that she needs more individualized attention that simply can't be met in a large classroom."

Blaze forced a calmness to his voice, despite how he felt. "I spoke to you before I enrolled her, and you said it wouldn't be a problem."

The principal held up his hand. "Mr. Warren, I said we would be patient and give her the opportunity to speak, but we're in the second half of the year and still nothing. She doesn't speak at all. We've done all we can with the school counselor, but we feel that Charlotte needs more specialized services beyond what we can offer here. If she spoke, we could get her into a small group for reading difficulties, but we tried that and she still didn't speak."

"But she writes and communicates in other ways. She's capable of speaking. She's just not ready." Blaze attempted to argue, but they didn't appear to want to listen. This was his daughter. He would make them listen. "If a teacher has a question, Charlotte can write down the answer."

"That isn't possible when the assignment is to read aloud. How will I assess her reading ability when she won't even open a book?" Ms. Miser folded her hands in her lap, and Blaze remembered that gaze that made him feel like he was a disappointment. "I know I expect a lot from my students, but when they leave my classroom, I want to know they are ready for fifth grade and beyond."

"I'll get her a tutor," Blaze offered, although he wasn't sure how he'd afford that right now.

Ms. Miser shook her head. "Mr. Warren, I'm afraid it goes beyond her ability to speak at this time. We've had some challenges with other students due to her being disrespectful when she refuses to open a book to follow along with me reading aloud. I've attempted to ask her why she won't open *Little Women* to follow along while I read to the class, but she won't respond. I know it might not seem like it, but I'm trying to help, and that's why I think she should be transferred to a school that is better equipped to handle her specific needs."

Tap. Tap. Tap.

They all looked to the opening door to find Jacqueline waltzing in as if she owned the entire town. She was stunning in her professional suit tailored to perfection around her hourglass frame.

"This is a closed meeting," Ms. Miser snipped at Jacqueline.

She didn't flinch or show any emotion at all. "I'm here because I believe I have a solution to this situation. If I may." She smiled and tilted her head in the angle that made the light shine in her eyes.

Principle Young tripped over the leg of his chair trying to stand. "Yes, please take my chair. What can you offer, Ms. Raynor?"

"This is highly irregular," Ms. Miser said, shifting in her seat. Jacqueline had been right. Ms. Miser was not happy to see her.

Jacqueline shook her head and placed a hand on the principal's shoulder, causing him to sit as if he were her puppet. Blaze had never seen a woman command such control in a room before.

"If the problem is about Charlotte's reading and Ms. Miser has a problem with her in class, perhaps it's because Charlotte is bored."

"Bored? I realize that the legendary Fabulous Five preferred entertainment over education in their youth, but this is a school meant for learning and I'm a teacher."

"No, that is not what I'm implying, although I do believe education could be more enjoyable. I'm referring to the fact that

Charlotte is beyond her grade level in reading, therefore she has had difficulty focusing."

Blaze lifted his chin, proud of his daughter because he'd witnessed her writing the dance list and knew what Jacqueline said was true.

"I understand that parents, and well, friends of the parents, want to believe their children are gifted, but I would know if Charlotte was beyond her reading level. Trust me, I've been a teacher a long time, and I've witnessed children regressing from reading groups because they are embarrassed or are lost because they are unable to follow along. I believe Charlotte is so far behind, she doesn't want anyone to know so she remains silent. That is why I think she needs to go somewhere that can catch her up to her grade level. It's what's best for her."

Jackie looked to Blaze and winked, sending his pulse into epileptic beating. "Principal Young, if I may demonstrate." She opened her purse and placed a piece of paper onto the desk. Blaze shifted Charlotte to the other knee and moved to the edge of the seat, where he saw that it was her list she'd made for the party.

"As you can see, Charlotte can not only read above her grade level, but she can write with perfect penmanship," Jacqueline announced to the room.

"That's impressive." Principal Young tapped the paper with his pointer finger and looked to Ms. Miser, as if that would end the debate.

"How do we know she wrote that and not someone else? It's obvious you both care for Charlotte, but you need to understand that you are not helping her by trying to keep her where she doesn't belong," Ms. Miser said in a calm but forceful tone. "Besides, you're not a relative or a caregiver, so you shouldn't be a part of this meeting. You know nothing of this child's abilities. It's secondhand information from your boyfriend."

"I assure you that Mr. Warren and I are not romantically

involved." Jacqueline lifted her chin a little too high, and Blaze didn't like it.

"Then who are you to Charlotte? What kind of authority do you have over this child's wellbeing?" Ms. Miser asked.

"I'm her nanny," Jacqueline stated as if it were fact.

Blaze opened his mouth to interject, but at the sight of Charlotte, he couldn't bring himself to burst her fairy-godmother-spotting smile.

Jacqueline turned to Charlotte. "Would you mind, honey, writing something for them? Perhaps you can write why you don't like to listen to Ms. Miser reading *Little Women* in class."

"I see Charlotte isn't the only one who shows disrespect," Ms. Miser said under her breath. The woman obviously still held ill feelings toward the Fabulous Five, especially Jacqueline. He had a feeling they had played a few too many pranks on her back in their day.

Blaze couldn't sit silent anymore. "I'd appreciate allowing Jacqueline the opportunity to show my daughter's talents instead of concentrating on her deficiencies."

Charlotte picked up the pen on the principal's desk and swallowed so loud that everyone in the room heard it.

Principal Young tapped the paper once more. "Go ahead, child."

Charlotte wrote for several minutes while Blaze held his breath.

When she was finished, the principal looked at the paper, then to Ms. Miser, and then at the rest of them. "Charlotte, would you do me a favor and wait outside for a couple of minutes while the rest of us finish speaking?"

The room remained quiet, but Jacqueline scooted Charlotte to the door and told her to wait in the main office. "As you can see, Principal Young, there is good reason why Charlotte doesn't listen to Ms. Miser in class, and you can see her level of writing is above average."

Ms. Miser huffed as if she were the fourth grader. "I don't see what writing has to do with listening to me read in class."

Principal Young's gaze changed from impartial to irritated. "Because, Ms. Miser, prior to Charlotte's arrival, she had read *Little Women*."

"So? That doesn't give her the right to not participate in class."

Principal Young cleared his throat and placed his glasses on his face before reading aloud, "Mommy read this story to me every night and promised we would be together always the way Marmie kept her family together."

Blaze felt like he'd fallen through the roof of a burning building. His poor little girl had suffered so much, and he planned on not allowing her to be punished for his mistakes any longer. "Principal Young, I'd like to request that my daughter be removed from Ms. Miser's class and placed in an advanced reading group. I'll continue to work with her at home."

"I will give Charlotte this opportunity, and I hope it will be what she needs. She'll be transferred today."

Blaze stood with his head held high and looked to Jacqueline, the woman who'd not only put a smile on his little girl's face but hope in his heart.

CHAPTER THIRTEEN

Jackie knelt in front of Charlotte outside the elementary school's main office and whispered, "You should've seen your father give it to Old Miser."

Charlotte looked up to her father with a questioning gaze.

"That's right. He took care of you, and you'll be moving up to the advanced reading class as of today." Jackie took the little girl's hands in hers and squeezed. "You're a smart girl. You'll do great."

Charlotte opened her mouth but then bowed her head. Jacqueline wanted to show her how loved she was so that she'd trust them enough to speak, but that would take time. In that moment, Jackie didn't want anything more in life than to help Charlotte. Perhaps even more than she'd wanted to prove herself worthy in New York and put her ex-husband back in his place. What had she done, saying she was the girl's nanny, though? She'd lost her ever-loving mind. The thought jolted her to move away, far away from this little thing that was distracting her from what mattered.

"Don't worry, darling. You won't have to speak until you're ready," Blaze told her in an I've-learned-to-speak-to-little-girls voice.

She lunged from the chair into his arms, wrapping her arms tightly around his neck.

The sight of the big, strong Blaze holding his little girl jump-started something inside Jackie. A piece of her she'd never known existed. When the fleeting thought of family and love shot through her, she made for the door, but before she could reach the threshold, Charlotte's little arms wrapped tight around her waist. The love poured through her into Jackie's resolve to keep her at a distance. Her insides melted.

"Go to class. You don't want to be late." Jackie nudged her from the embrace and sent her on her way and then bolted to the nearest exit.

Blaze chased her down before she could reach the outer doors. "Where're you going?"

"I've got a meeting to save the dance with the Fabulous Five, remember?" Her heels tapped, tapped, tapped, but she wasn't fast enough.

Blaze jogged ahead and blocked her escape. "Wait, talk to me. What is it? I can tell you're freaked out, and I don't know what I did this time. I only want to thank you for helping Charlotte like that. You were amazing. I've never known a woman with such…such—"

"Determination?"

"Yes, but more than that." His gaze bounced around the hall as if he'd spot the words written in swirling letters on a chalkboard.

She eyed the sunlight outside, longing for a deep breath of fresh air beyond the stale, antiseptic smell of the school. "Attitude?"

"No."

"Sassiness?" Wait, that was Stella, not her. "Rudeness?"

"No. Passion."

She almost fell off her heels the way he breathed the word and looked at her as if she were his savior. She'd never been a person to help anyone but herself. This wasn't her role. It was his.

"You're the hero, not me. I only had a solution to a problem and I shared it."

His hands gripped her arms, not tight but in a firm way that told her he wanted her to listen. Children skittered around behind them going to their classes. He backed her from the door as it swung open with little ones running before they were late. All the motion distracted her. He leaned in and pressed his strong lips to her cheek and then whispered, "Thank you."

The warm breath over her ear and the commotion around her made her dizzy. Her belly fluttered like chiffon in a tornado. A man hadn't been that close since she was married. Her ex had grown bored of her and moved on to the next victim. No. This wasn't right. She didn't want to feel this…this hunger inside her that only lead to pain and disappointment.

She cleared her throat and shoved past him. "I need to go. I'll be late."

"Did you mean it? Are you going to be their nanny?"

She didn't answer him. She only rushed to her car in record speed, closed the roof on her convertible, and turned the heat to full blast, trying to stop the shaking in her body. With her foot pressed to the gas, she fled from the school, from the emotions, from Elijah "Blaze" Warren—who turned her around and made her forget what was important, who'd dragged her into his life and cracked the door on her heart open for his children.

That wasn't her. She needed to refocus. She'd get the dresses made and save the dance and then move on before she got too attached to the little monsters. She'd only cared about them because they were into fashion and because Tabitha worshiped her. It had been a long time since someone had worshiped her. What had Jackie's mother always told her? *It is better to be worshiped than loved because love fades but fame lasts for centuries.*

She swung into a parking space and bolted into Maple Grounds with her emotions locked tight and her determination to finish a job in place. "Hello, girls. Let's get started."

"Oh no, hold up a minute." Stella leaned back and propped her ugly, dark combat boots up on Mary-Beth's clean table. Based on the way the Coffee Whisperer looked at Stella, she wasn't happy either.

Felicia gently pushed her boots off the table and eyed everyone with that oh-no-it's-about-to-explode tight-faced look.

"No time. I have a busy day. I'll need both you and Carissa at my shop this afternoon to work on your dresses. Got it? For now, let's concentrate on—"

"You liking Blaze?" Stella overstepped and slid off the friendship runway into the pit of gossip.

"I'm not going to pretend to like someone so I can further your fiancé's career, so stop. You should be ashamed of yourself for trying to manipulate me into thinking I like him and those girls anyway. You're the one who put the idea in my head. This is your fault." She slammed her bag down on the table and faced the girls, who all looked at her with soft faces and mouths open. "What are you all looking at? I told you, we have work to do."

"Hon, you know we love you," Felicia said.

"Whatever. Can we get to work now or what?" Her shirt and bra felt constricting, like it squeezed the breath from her lungs, and she found herself fighting for air.

Mary-Beth scooted the mug toward Jackie, so she took a sip to give herself a minute to calm down. The warmth of chamomile slid down her throat and soothed her lungs, as if nudging them open once more. She took a breath and set the cup down. How did Mary-Beth always know what someone needed in a beverage? She'd never served Jackie tea before two in the afternoon before. The girl really was a coffee, or more accurately, beverage whisperer.

Carissa eyed everyone, and Jackie tried to catch the bopping gazes of communication in a language she obviously didn't understand. "Stop it. All of you. Stop doing that thing where you all know what you're talking about but me. It weirds me out."

"Jackie, we know you're upset." Carissa reached for her, but Jackie yanked her arm away.

"Of course I'm upset. Stella is still trying to push Blaze and me together."

"I'm not," Stella said in a don't-push-me-too-far tone.

"If that's how you want to cope… But just know we are all here for you when you want to talk about it," Felicia said, leaning in to catch Jackie's gaze.

"About what? Mary-Beth, what did you put in everyone's drink today? Crazy sugar?" Jackie opened her bag and removed her phone and list.

When no one said anything, Jackie huffed. "Fine, then let's move forward. What about the dance?" Tabitha must've changed her phone's wallpaper, because it was a picture of the two girls with Blaze from yesterday. They must've shot it when she was busy doing something else. Her insides warmed at the sight of their smiling faces dressed in hats and fancy clothes. They'd put the pretty summer hat with the purple ribbon on top of Blaze's head. She couldn't help but laugh at the sight.

"That," Stella said in a voice Jackie would swear almost sounded comforting. She pointed to Jackie's phone, and Jackie looked up to find three other heads nodding their agreement.

"What? This?" Jackie dropped her phone as if it were about to catch fire. "I didn't put that picture on my phone. That was all Tabitha. She's a teenage girl who needs to be taught personal space, that's all."

Jackie retrieved her phone once more, willing this conversation to end and to focus on the dance, on the jobs that needed to be completed, on the future, not some fantasy but reality. But her hands shook and her body trembled. "Now let's focus."

"I have an idea," Carissa said with her gaze secured to Stella.

"What is it?" Mary-Beth asked.

"Spit it out," Stella ordered.

"If Stella doesn't hate the idea, why don't we combine the

school dance and the wedding reception? I mean, considering it's part of the Knox Brevard show, the entire town will be invited anyway. We'll use the royalty theme, and everyone can come as a royal couple or person."

Everyone sat quietly and watched Stella study the grease under her nails. "If Knox is on board, I'm cool with it. It'll combine funds, and everyone can chip in since it's a town event. That way, the parents and kids from the school don't have to come up with all the money."

"I think it's a great idea." Mary-Beth jingled her bracelets as if adding an exclamation point to her agreement.

"I'll run it by the girls and let you all know." Jackie didn't hate the idea. It actually was a good way to handle it. The town always came together when it counted.

"What will you and Blaze wear to the party?" Stella teased.

"Never going to happen. We are not meant to be together, so you can drop it. I'm not interested. I'm only interested in making my way back to New York." Jackie clutched her phone so tight, she thought she'd crack the screen.

The screen they all stared at once again.

"Hon, your parents did a number on you, and you've been hiding all these years behind faux relationships and working to be someone important because that's what you were taught. But trust us, this could be something that makes you happy. Not superficial enjoyment from a job well done, but truly, unequivocally, over-the-moon happy."

Felicia's words pounded at Jackie's head, her heart, her soul, but she found them absurd. "You do realize this is the one man I would never choose to have in my life. I'll never have children, I've never liked children, and I prefer my life unattached."

The girls all nodded passively, but she knew they wanted to say more. Only, she wouldn't listen. "Now, let's get to work."

CHAPTER FOURTEEN

"Jacqueline's going to be our new nanny?" Tabitha shouted only seconds after she was tucked into Blaze's truck and he was leaving the high school. He dared a quick glance at her and found a note written in Charlotte's writing in her hands.

How did he handle the question? He didn't know if she was truly committed to the job since she'd run off so fast. "Well, I don't know."

"Come on, Dad. You're the one who insists that we need someone to stay with us. Now you're going to take away the only nanny we want?"

"No," he said flatly. He didn't want to always be the bad guy. He wanted to protect his daughters, but they weren't going to believe him even if he told them she couldn't do it. And he wasn't even sure if she was or wasn't serous. "I have no problem with her watching you girls."

Charlotte bounced in her seat clapping, and Tabitha squealed.

He wanted to warn them about the situation, how Jacqueline had run out and he wasn't sure she'd meant what she'd said in the principal's office, but what if he was wrong? What if Jacqueline did want to be with them at night? Then he'd really be the villain if he told them otherwise. "I think we should go to the shop to make sure this is all ironed out."

"Don't talk her out of it, please," Tabitha begged.

Blaze turned down the road to head into town. "I won't even speak. I'll let you talk to Ms. Raynor about it. Just remember, sometimes adults say things in the moment and discover later they've over committed themselves. I just don't want you to be disappointed, that's all."

Tabitha and Charlotte communicated with each other in a way only sisters could without words. "I won't be," Tabitha said firmly and Charlotte nodded.

Blaze worried all the way to the parking behind Jacqueline's shop that his girls were about to get their little hearts broken again. He shouldn't do this. He should protect them, but how could he? They were determined to believe he was the one who'd pushed Jacqueline away, but in reality she was running.

The girls flew out of the truck and slammed the door before he managed to cut the engine. "Wait."

They were inside the shop before he reached the bottom step, and part of him didn't want to go in and face Tabitha and Charlotte being let down, but he did. Because someone would need to pick them up when they were disappointed.

With a heavy weight in his chest, he opened the door and entered to find his daughters jumping up and down around Carissa, Stella, and Jacqueline. She looked up at him with a tense set to her jaw before Charlotte yanked her sleeve to look at her.

"I can't believe you said you'd be our nanny. We're so excited. We promise to brush our teeth, help with dinner and dishes, and go to bed without an argument. We'll be the best two girls you've ever taken care of," Tabitha squealed.

"You would be the only two girls I've ever taken care of." She softened her face and cupped Charlotte's chin. "I'm not sure I'm qualified for such a job. I was trying to help, but I'm afraid Ms.

Miser got under my skin and I said some things before I thought about it."

"Wait, Dad was right?" Tabitha backed away, pulling Charlotte with her. "You lied? You don't want to be our nanny?"

"Lied? No." Jacqueline shuffled forward, but they backed away farther.

Blaze jumped to their side. "Don't worry, girls. We'll figure something out. I've gotcha."

"All I meant was that I should've asked you girls first before I blurted something out like that without thinking."

"Yeah, she should think before she opens her mouth," Stella said, loud enough for all to hear, but Jacqueline obviously ignored her.

"Yay! I can't wait. We'll play dress-up and read stories and talk about boys." Tabitha looked at Blaze as if she just remembered he was standing there. "I told Dad you wouldn't let us down."

Charlotte flung her arms around Jacqueline's waist, and Blaze saw fear, the kind that would take a grown man to the ground. Were the rumors true? If so, why did Jacqueline hate children so much?

Stella and Carissa broke apart from a little personal conversation and joined them. "Hey, Jackie tells me that she designed dresses for you. Can I see them?" Carissa asked.

"Can we show her?" Tabitha asked.

"Of course." Jacqueline looked to him and then at the girls.

Stella approached him. "Hey, I forgot to call you back. Now a good time to check that problem you've been having with the truck?"

He didn't even have a chance to ask her what she was talking about before she grabbed him by the arm and yanked him toward the door.

"Good, 'cause I'm busy tomorrow."

She didn't stop until she'd dragged him down the steps and stopped at the side of his truck. "Pop the hood."

"What? I don't have a problem, and if I did I'm sure I could fix it."

"Yeah, well, I'm not here to fix your truck, but if you don't open that hood and Jackie catches on that I pulled you out here to give you the backstory on why she's the way she is, then she'll break both of us."

He mindlessly opened the hood and joined her at the front, where they were shielded from a prying Jacqueline eyeing them through the window.

"Okay, listen up. You couldn't have chosen a more pain in the neck, high-strung person to fall in love with."

"I'm not—"

She shot up a hand at him. "She's also the most loving, caring, amazing, talented person you could ever meet. And if you tell her I said that, I'll fix your truck so it'll never run again. Got me?"

"Ah, gotcha."

"She's broken. Her parents pulled a real psycho trip on her. They paraded her around and made her feel like the only thing she could ever contribute to the world was being beautiful. Children were a waste of time and they ruined your body and your life was what her mother would say while dragging her to modeling jobs that barely paid while her father started Jacqueline on her own modeling career. It wasn't until she ran off with Carissa's ex after high school that she broke free. I believe she did it to sabotage ever returning to Sugar Maple, but after her parents left for good and Ms. Horton called her back, she returned even more broken than when she'd left. I'll let her tell you about her scumbag of an ex-husband, but for now, know the girl is nothing but an angel in devil's clothing."

"What's going on out there?" Jacqueline called from the doorway.

"Almost done," she shouted. Then she continued just for his ears. "Remember, just because someone is broken, it doesn't mean they're worthless."

If anyone could understand that, it was Blaze. His ex-wife had done a number on him, too. Broken and pushing people away, he could understand. How to fix it wasn't.

Stella closed the hood with a bang. "That should do it." She wiped her hands down her jeans and looked up at Jacqueline. "Like what you're thinking for my wedding dress. Remember, no lace."

Carissa shot through the door and past Jacqueline. "We best go so these two can work out the details on the nanny situation." She waved to them both and joined Stella at a fast pace toward the center of town.

He stood there feeling like he was at a crossroad and needed to make a decision. Did he go inside and speak with Jacqueline and ask her about her past and confess his own? No, not tonight, because tonight only one thing mattered. He marched into the store and took her to the back office. "Did you mean it? Are you going to watch the girls for me?"

"For now. But keep looking for another nanny. I'll explain that I'm working to leave town soon and that I want them to have a long-term solution."

"Leaving town?" he asked, a sting shooting through him.

Jacqueline straightened her waist-cinching belt and stood tall. "It's always been my plan. Once the bridal dresses are done and the Knox Brevard segment on my shop airs, I hope it will put me on the fast track to return to New York City."

Her words were like a forest fire of sadness that spread quickly and destroyed everything in its path.

CHAPTER FIFTEEN

Storyboards, spreadsheets, photos, and documents littered Jackie's glass table in her shop. Knox and Stella were sitting shoulder to shoulder as if they wouldn't be able to breathe if they weren't touching. Jackie had made a play for Knox when he'd first arrived in town, but now she saw how perfect Stella was for him. They were inseparable. Jackie hadn't been able to get a moment alone with Stella to ask her what she discussed with Blaze. She'd been so obvious, the way she'd dragged the man outside and hidden behind the hood of his truck. She had half a mind to stop the meeting and ask her in front of everyone what she was doing alone with Blaze outside.

Drew and Carissa were snuggled on the other side of the table, and their assistant Lori sat across from Jacqueline with the same feeling-like-a-fifth-wheel expression.

"So what do you think?" Knox asked, but Jacqueline didn't know what he was talking about. She'd been eyeing the door, waiting for Blaze to walk in with the two girls she'd be charged with all night. She was scared, not of watching them but of the fact she'd woken this morning with a want to do so.

"Jackie?" Knox shuffled the papers and nudged some toward her.

She acted like she was analyzing them, but she didn't have the mental capacity to decipher what was in front of her. Not when her world had been turned upside down by a firefighter and two little minions. "Fine."

"Fine?" Knox asked, his eyebrows raised, and she knew he was irritated but had no clue why.

"Yes, you've done a great job. I look forward to working with you."

"It's true… Jacqueline Raynor's been tamed by a man and two children." Knox reached for the papers. Perhaps he was upset that he wasn't able to tame her. No, Stella was the right woman for him, not that Jackie would ever admit it aloud.

Stella covered his hand. "Great, so it's settled. Your kiss with Blaze next to the two wedding dresses on the mannequins will be our promo reel?"

"What?" Jackie's body turned stone hard and cold. "I-I didn't agree to that."

Drew cleared his throat. "How would you know? You've been looking at that door this entire meeting. Who you waiting for?"

They all snickered and looked at one another.

"I'm not a joke. This is my business, and you're not going to pervert it by parading around a faux romance."

"Pervert? Is that what you think of love?" Carissa asked.

That was it. "Meeting's over." Jackie rose with the dignity of a lady and strutted to her office. She would not stoop to her old ways of lashing out or insulting others. Instead, she'd simply walked away.

"Let's resume tomorrow," Lori said from the other room, allowing Jackie to take a breath and sit in her desk chair to relax for a moment. She rubbed her temples and closed her eyes.

"Tomorrow we need to finish. The film crew will be here in a few days. I need the dresses done, the storyboard approved, filming locations, permits—" Knox's words caused Jackie's nerves to ignite in a frenzy of anxiety.

"Don't worry. We have connections," Stella said in her rarely used noncombative voice.

Jacqueline heard the front door open and close, allowing her a minute of peace, so she picked up her pen and scribbled a list of what she needed to complete.

- Design dresses approval.
- Check fabric order.
- Notions order.
- Review storyboard.
- Bead Tabitha's dress.

Wait, no. This was business. It wasn't about the girls. She scribbled lines through the last entry and tapped her pen on the desk.

"Can we come in?" Carissa knocked on the open door. Jackie looked up to find Carissa and Lori bunched together with only their toes daring to enter the room.

Great. They hadn't left. "I don't know. Is Stella going to try to shove this pretend love story on me any more?"

Lori waltzed in and sat on the sage settee against the other wall as if she were at home instead of Jackie's office. "We sent her away. It's just us nice girls for now."

Drew's assistant had fast become an extended member of the Fabulous Five since she was around the same age and always seemed to care about the town.

"You can stay, then."

"Whatcha working on?" Carissa asked, joining Lori on the settee.

"A list."

Carissa scratched her temple. "I figured it was a list, but what list is it and why did you murder the last line?"

Jackie noticed she'd put a hole in the paper the way she felt like there was a hole inside of her. A big, black, imploding hole that seemed to threaten to turn her inside out when it came to Tabitha and Charlotte. "Because it didn't belong on this list. That's all."

"Because you only write the most important details on a list," Lori said.

"Right."

Carissa tilted her head and gave her inquisitive expression a try, but Jackie saw through it as the intrusion that it was. "So that last one wasn't important to you?"

Jackie crumpled the paper and threw it into the trash, realizing where Carissa was going with her line of questioning. "Actually, I'm done making lists." She swiveled her chair to face the girls. "You know, you will actually need to wear heels and do your hair for the wedding instead of living in jeans and a Sugar and Soul Bakery T-shirt." Jackie had tried so hard not to use her shield of insults to protect herself anymore, but they were pushing too hard.

"I look forward to it." Carissa eyed the trash bin as if she could read that final line if she focused hard enough.

They all sat quietly for a moment, and Jackie knew they were itching to ask or tell her something. "Spit it out."

"What?" Carissa asked in her apple tartlet sweet tone.

Lori snapped her fingers as if a moment of realization had struck. "That's what I admire about you—straight to the point always. Fine, we have a question for you."

"Okay." Jackie sat straight, pushing her shoulders back. "Go ahead."

"I think you might have missed something in the meeting, and I wanted to make sure you were ready for it this weekend," Lori spoke as if to a child.

Jackie rotated her hand at the wrist in a move-along signal.

"You agreed to show the dresses to the girls next Saturday live on the Knox Brevard show. That means a photo shoot and filming," Lori said, still talking to her as if the real news was yet to come.

"And?" Jackie asked.

"Knox asked Blaze to be in it, too."

Jackie burst into laughter. "Seriously, he'll never agree to that. And no, I'm not going to convince him for you."

Carissa stood, crossed the small space, and put a hand on her shoulder as if to hold her in her seat. "He already did."

Jackie shook her head. "No way he'd do that. He didn't even want the girls on screen. What's changed?"

Carissa shrugged.

"Stella. What did she say to him? I know you're all in cahoots together." Before Jackie could interrogate the truth out of them, the front door squeaked open.

"Hello?" Blaze's deep voice echoed from the store into her office and under her skin.

"Go ask him yourself." Lori pointed toward the front.

Jackie stood, smoothed her skirt down, fluffed her hair, and waltzed out to find the girls and Blaze with expectant gazes.

Charlotte ran over and hugged her tightly around the waist. Tabitha approached but stopped a few steps away. "She wanted me to tell you that she is super excited about tonight and that she won't be a bother at all."

Jackie looked to Blaze. What was going on with him? He'd flipped from distant to fully accepting her in their lives overnight. Okay, that wasn't fair. He didn't act that way, but he sure seemed to warm to the idea of her around his kids way too fast.

Blaze stepped forward in his fireman t-shirt and pants. How could a simple outfit scream sexy hero when it was mass produced in a factory? Yet somehow, it did, and Jackie's breath apparently noticed, given the way it quickened. This needed to stop. Now. "Right, we'll close up shop in a bit and then head to your house. Before we go, I need to review some house rules with your dad. For now, I need you two to go try on your dresses for a proper fitting." She pointed to the dressing room, and the girls flew past, dropping their backpacks at her feet.

Carissa and Lori swished by them without even a word until they reached the table. "We need to go. Chat with you tomorrow. Good luck tonight."

Lori paused by her bag. "Oh, before I forget. Mary-Beth said she didn't need these anymore and assumed you would." She set a brown paper bag in the chair and followed Carissa out the front door.

Jackie didn't pause long enough to see what was in the bag. She needed to have a friendly chat with fireman Blaze before the girls returned. "What's going on with you? You went from distant to in my face with the girls. You said you didn't want them hurt again, but you told them I'd be their nanny. You obviously didn't let them know that I wasn't staying in Sugar Maple, which means they'll get hurt. I thought you were Mr. Overprotective. What gives?"

Blaze didn't react the way she'd expected. Instead of a stern, I'm-in-charge stare, he sat down at the table and stretched his leg out. "I'm done being the bad guy."

"What's that supposed to mean?"

"It means, I'm not the one who'll tell them you're leaving. Those two girls are finally settling in. I heard Charlotte whisper when I was in the room this morning. Despite how I feel about you being in their lives, you're good for them. As for the future, who knows when you'll leave. There are rumors that you won't be leaving at all."

Jackie threw her hands up in the air. "Seriously? That's what Stella stole you away to tell you? The other members of the Fabulous Five will do anything to sabotage me returning to New York because they want me to stay here. They think I don't get it. They believe that the Knox Brevard show is supposed to shower me with success and I'll decide I don't want to leave Sugar Maple, but that's not it. I'm using the show to expand my career and make my way back into the fashion world. News flash, that isn't here. It's not with you."

"No one said anything about me." Blaze's I-knew-you-liked-me grin enraged her.

"It's not with your girls, either. I'm not staying, not for the Fabulous Five, not for you, and not for those girls."

Sniff. Sniff. Sniff.

Jackie swung around to find Charlotte standing behind her with tears streaming down her face. Out of all the things Jackie had done wrong in her life to protect herself from the world, this was the worst, most selfish thing ever. And she would've given her dreams to take back her words and wipe those tears away.

CHAPTER SIXTEEN

Blaze tried to remain calm, to give Jacqueline a chance after what he'd found out about her past, but she had crushed his baby girl. "Come on, girls. We should go. I'll call in sick tonight, and we'll figure something out tomorrow."

"No. Wait." To Blaze's surprise, Jacqueline didn't look defensive or angry. She looked broken. It was the first crack he'd seen in her armor, and he wanted to break it away and comfort her. A foreign notion to a man who wanted to keep real feelings at a distance. But her prima donna façade crumbled in front of him, and the raw sight of the real Jacqueline Raynor did something to him.

"Why should we?" he asked in that talk-to-girls voice he'd adopted.

Tabitha settled firmly on the side of the room with him, but Charlotte remained in neutral territory. She wanted the love of a woman in her life so much, she couldn't face being rejected again. What would this do to her ability to speak? He had no one to blame but himself. He should have kept them safe.

"We still need to do the fitting," Tabitha said in a shaky voice, as if she wasn't sure herself that the dress meant that much to her. And if he was right, that dress meant everything in her teenage world.

Charlotte turned and pointed to her zipper. He wanted to scoop her up in his arms, dress and all, and run from the store. But before he had a chance to move, Jacqueline took a chair and dragged it to them and sat down facing Charlotte, who had covered her face in her hands as if to hide from the world.

"Listen, I know I hurt your feelings, and I'm sorry. You see, I was scared."

Blaze's fatherly instinct kicked in, and he wanted to take the girls and go, to save them the heartbreak, but he waited to see how Charlotte and Tabitha would react to Jacqueline's statement.

Charlotte peered from under her hands, allowing one eye to show.

"What were you scared of?" Tabitha asked.

His gut knotted. Darn if he didn't want to know himself, but not at the expense of his girls.

"Of you two. At caring for you both too much. You see, I always try to leave before someone can leave me."

Her words slashed through Blaze's resolve, and he paused his retreat at the sight of the way she sat with hunched shoulders and a wandering gaze, broken and alone. "Like both of you, I've suffered the feeling of abandonment. Maybe that's why I couldn't help but tell Ms. Miser and Principal Young that I was your nanny. I wanted to protect you the way no one ever protected me."

"Are you leaving us?" Tabitha asked in a sterile tone.

Jacqueline sighed. "I promise that I will always tell you the truth and that I'll never abandon you, but that doesn't mean that I'll always stay in Sugar Maple. At the moment, I hope to use the Knox Brevard show to put myself on the national fashion radar again. You see, my ex-husband stole my designs and my business and then shamed me into leaving New York City. I came back here to figure out my life, and then I'd planned to return when it was the right time."

"But you have this shop and your friends," Tabitha said, as if that were all Jacqueline ever would need in life. But he knew she had to prove herself to the world.

"My friends are getting married and moving on with their lives. I need to do the same."

"You could marry Dad," Tabitha said in the most sincere tone.

"That's enough," he said, careful not to use his deep voice. "I know you two are upset, and you have no idea how much I want to make all your pain go away, but Jacqueline agreed to nanny for you, not to be your mother. Do you both want her to be around until she leaves, or do you want me to find a different person to watch you while I'm at work?"

"I hope you say you want me, because I was looking forward to spending time with you both. We were going to have a fashion show and hot chocolate and talk about boys."

"We could skip the last part," Blaze half joked.

"Oh, Dad." Tabitha rolled her eyes.

Charlotte pointed to Jacqueline, giving her approval for the night. Tabitha took Charlotte by the hand and led her toward the pedestal to do their dress fitting. "We'll stay with Ms. Raynor tonight, and we can decide tomorrow. You can go to work for now, Dad. We'll be fine." Tabitha sounded too grown-up for her years, while Charlotte looked too young for her age.

He eyed the door, Jacqueline, and his daughters and knew one thing… He still had no idea what the right decision was. He'd thought he was starting to get the hang of parenting, but apparently he wasn't.

"Go, we'll be fine." Jacqueline stood, her gaze everywhere but on him. She appeared…embarrassed, but why?

"Go, Dad, before you're late for work," Tabitha ordered.

"Okay." He looked to Jacqueline. "Walk me out?"

She nodded and said to the girls, "Wait for me at the stage, and I'll be back to pin the hem of the dresses."

Blaze went out the back door and held it open for Jacqueline. "Can we speak for a moment?"

She followed him to a safe distance from the shop so the girls couldn't hear them.

"I know you've been through a lot in your life, but I have to protect my girls. Will you be able to watch them for a few days and perhaps allow me to find a new nanny, and then you can slowly distance yourself from them? I think having you leave abruptly would hurt them worse."

"Of course. They're darling children. I'm just not good with kids." Jacqueline's gaze remained downcast, and Blaze didn't like seeing such a strong woman broken.

"Who says? As far as I can tell, you're great with them."

She sighed. "Listen, I'll stay until you can find someone. They're better off without me. I'm poison. I don't know how to be a role model for young women. Trust me. I'm not the one you want your kids aspiring to be."

Blaze moved in, ready to make her see what he saw. He tipped her chin up to make her look at him, despite the fact he worried she'd slug him. "Listen to me. People don't know the real you because you've put up such a show to protect yourself from harm. Based on the little I know about your life, it's understandable. Maybe it's time for you to start opening yourself up to possibilities."

"You don't understand."

"I do." Blaze ignored the warning sparking like an electric fire to keep his truth to himself, but he'd be a hypocrite if he did. What kind of father would he be if he couldn't speak the truth to someone who needed to hear it? "I know because I've done similar things. Dating women who mean nothing to me or avoiding people and relationships all together because I blame myself for the failure of my marriage. What if I'm not good enough? I wasn't good enough to handle a wife who woke up one day and decided she wanted me to change everything about myself and if I didn't she'd have a breakdown. I gave up my friends, my cars, my hobbies all to make her happy, but in the end it wasn't enough. I wasn't enough." He choked on the raw emotion of it, not wanting to look like less than a man in front of Jacqueline.

"I'm sorry." She cupped his cheek and moved in close, so close he could feel her breath on his chin. "I, too, have never been good enough to keep people in my life. In your case, though, you did everything you could. All I do is push them away."

He squeezed her arms and rested his head to hers. Could he have found a woman he could truly understand? A woman as broken as him?

CHAPTER SEVENTEEN

The Warren home was warm but masculine throughout until Jackie reached Tabitha and Charlotte's rooms with pops of girly stuff. Still, the walls and décor were too bland for little girls.

Jackie reheated the casserole that Blaze had made. Apparently the man could cook, but the note on the top said, *Don't tell my men if you like this. I have them convinced I don't know a spatula from a drill.*

She liked being in on a secret. There was a family warmth to the home that she'd never felt before, a comfortable, lived-in feel. Of course, it could use a little woman's touch.

Tabitha sat at the kitchen table working on her homework while Charlotte read silently in the oversize recliner by the stone-stacked fireplace. Jackie could imagine hot cocoa in front of the roaring fire on a cold night, snuggled up next to Blaze and the children.

She dropped the serving spoon into the sink with a loud clank, drawing both girls' attention. "Sorry, it slipped." What was wrong with her? Was her biological clock ticking? She'd thought she didn't even have a clock. She shook off the dangerous wayward thoughts and sat down to work on finishing the sketches for Stella's and Carissa's wedding dresses, since the fabric and notions should be arriving in the next few days.

That's what she needed to focus on, the show and her future.

Tabitha hit her head against the table twice.

"What is it?"

"Math. I hate the subject. There's no point to it. Why will I ever need to know this stuff anyway?"

Jackie smiled. "More than you'd think."

"Really?" She propped her head on her hand and eyed the algebraic expressions.

"Sure. Let's say I want to make a dress, but I only have so much fabric to use. I've got to make sure I cut precisely by measuring everything and figuring out the best way to lay out the pieces to maximize the fabric. To do that, you use geometry and algebra."

"Okay, but that's less math than all of these complicated calculations."

"Yes, but running a business of any kind, you need to understand debits, credits, how to manage to stretch your dollar as far as you can. Math is an integral part of my business. If I hadn't taken accounting, algebra, and other math classes, I wouldn't be able to run my store today."

"I hadn't thought about it that way." Tabitha picked up her pencil and studied the problems in front of her. "Okay, so I can see how I could use this equation in business." It took Tabitha a few tries, but Jackie watched her work through the problem until she found the correct answer.

"That's great. You've got it."

"If I think of it like you said, as a problem for a business, it's more interesting."

Charlotte hopped down from the chair and pointed at the clock.

"It's her bath and bedtime," Tabitha announced.

Jackie paused, not sure what to do with a little girl's bedtime routine, but she was a smart woman and there was no reason to fear Charlotte. "Let's get a bath drawn, then. Do you like bubbles?"

Charlotte clapped and jumped up and down in affirmation. For the next hour, she sat in the bathroom while Charlotte played with the bubbles, giggling aloud. She had the most intoxicating laugh that made Jacqueline close her eyes and just listen.

Once, she'd longed to hear the sounds of horns and sirens and shouting of the city, but this was the next best thing. For now.

When Charlotte's bath turned cold, Jackie wrapped her in a big towel and sent her to dress for bed in her princess nightgown. Before Jackie could clean up the bathroom, Charlotte handed her a brush and pulled the hair tie, letting her blonde curls fall down her back. The girl's hair was the color of Cinderella's and as soft as cashmere.

They sat on her bed, and Jackie brushed 100 times while Charlotte sat still until she was done.

"Okay, time for bed." Jackie pulled back the covers to find some princess sheets and an old worn bear. Charlotte slid under the covers and pulled them to her neck. "Night, sweet girl."

Jackie returned to the kitchen to check on Tabitha and found her smiling down at her paper. "I did it. I think I got them all right all on my own."

"Of course you did." Jackie offered her proudest smile.

"I'm not the smart one. I'm more the creative type. Charlotte is actually super smart. She takes after my mom." The way Tabitha's light faded in her eyes made Jackie want to pull her in for a hug.

"I promise you're smart. I can tell. You're as bright as they come, and you can do anything when you work hard. You remind me of myself at your age."

"Really?"

"Yes. I struggled in school, but when I found my passion for fashion, everything changed. It was as if everything made more sense."

She smiled and closed her book, but then that same darkness shadowed over her. "Do you think children can catch things from their parents? Like hereditary wise?"

Jacqueline felt the weight of her question and thought it was a conversation Tabitha should have with her father, not Jackie herself.

"I think my mother suffers from mental illness. Does that mean Charlotte will?"

The raw honesty of her question shot through Jackie, and she had to sit down before she fell. "I hope not." Jackie willed herself to share something that she'd never said aloud before. "That would mean that I'd be like my mother. A woman who only cared about fame and fortune and never found happiness. A woman who never once put her child before herself. A woman who was never fulfilled in life."

"Then I know we don't have to be like our mothers. Because you're nothing like that." Tabitha hugged her, causing Jackie to stiffen at the sudden intrusion, but then she softened and placed a hand on Tabitha's back.

"Be careful not to put me on a pedestal. I'm not worthy of your admiration—unless it has to do with fashion."

Jackie felt something strange, a fullness she'd never experienced in life. She brushed it off as a moment until Charlotte entered the room and held out a book. Not just any book, but *Little Women*. The book that her mother once read to her. Jackie pulled Charlotte into the hug and whispered, "I'd be honored to read if you'd like."

Before Jackie knew how to stop herself, they'd all crawled into Charlotte's bed, snuggled together, and read *Little Woman* together. Like a mother would to her girls.

CHAPTER EIGHTEEN

The fire truck squealed to a halt out front of Blaze's home. Blaze was forever grateful that the men didn't mind stopping by his house on the way to the grocery store so he could check on his girls. He entered the house with shoes off, tiptoeing on the hardwood floor to Charlotte's room.

He nudged the door open to find more than just his little girl asleep in bed. Instead, he found Jacqueline wrapped around them, one on each arm, resembling a Michelangelo painting—beautiful, breathtaking, bewildering. A sight so perfect it couldn't be real. The only thing missing was himself. But Jacqueline wasn't his girl. She had plans to leave, to run off to New York. A place he didn't and would never belong. He was a small-town man. He'd tried to live in DC for Angela's sake, but he'd hated every minute in that noisy place, where no one even said hello when they passed by on the streets. He enjoyed everything about his small town and the residents. The big city was great to visit, but it wasn't home.

He stood there for several minutes watching them sleep, unable to tear his eyes away. Until his radio blared, stirring them all. He retreated at full run to the fire truck, welcoming a distraction of combating flames.

To his relief and disappointment, the home fire was only a clogged flue on someone's fireplace. Why they were lighting a fire on such a beautiful spring day, he couldn't fathom, but he didn't ask. Instead, he returned to the firehouse with his men.

"You've got it bad, man," Marco announced to the men removing their fire gear and placing it in their designated spots.

"What?" Blaze shook off the image of the sleeping princesses that stuck in his head and faced four men gawking at him.

"You're right. The last bachelor of the bunch is about to lose his freedom," David shouted, as if the men weren't three feet apart.

The rest laughed and joked and teased, but Blaze ignored them. "I'll get breakfast started."

"Whoa, hold up. Blaze is volunteering to cook? What's up with that?" Captain Taylor followed him into the kitchen, and Blaze prepared for a good ragging from the guys.

He snatched food from the fridge. "How do you men want your eggs?"

"Sunny side up of information. Is this about Jacqueline Raynor? The snotty girl who walks around town like she owns everything and everyone?" Marco walked like a linebacker on heels, swaying his hips.

"She's not like that," Blaze snapped before he realized he'd opened a window for these men to climb into his personal business.

"And there it is. The man has no hope." David sat with one butt cheek on the table.

"I'm too busy with work and my girls to even consider a relationship right now."

"Relationship? One date and Blaze is talking relationships now." Marco high-fived David. He was probably still mad about not including him on the carpentry job.

"No, I'm not. I've never even been on a date with Jacqueline."

"Well, at least he admits it's her." Tom snagged a bottle of water from the fridge and stood by Blaze as if he'd get some sort of information through osmosis.

Blaze glowered at him. "Probie, you're not in this conversation."

Captain Taylor cleared his throat. "Guess they want to help cook since they're in the kitchen."

With that one sentence, the men scattered faster than a flame caught on dry hay.

Blaze decided to scramble a big pan of eggs and tossed some bacon in another to make it easy. The men wouldn't complain since the rule dictated if they didn't like something, then they were the next to cook. "Thanks. I'm not in the mood to be razzed by the men right now."

"I can understand that." Captain Taylor pulled out a chair and sat as if staying for a while. "You know, Jacqueline is a beautiful woman. You can't deny that."

"No, I guess not." Blaze whipped the eggs and added some milk, salt, and chopped some vegetables. "But she's only watching my girls until I can find a full-time nanny."

"She's been good for you, too," Captain said, ignoring his words.

Blaze realized if he wanted this conversation to end, he had to allow it to happen. Captain never walked away until he made his point. "In what way?" Blaze kept his attention on the chopping so he didn't have to face his captain and his words.

"She's softened the rough edges, which can only help when raising two girls. Trust me, I know. I have four."

"I guess." He beat the mixture until it bubbled and then poured it into the prepared pan.

"And you want to keep your girls, right?"

"Yes," Blaze shouted more than said.

"And they'll have a choice if your ex-wife decides she's had enough alone time with her new boyfriend? They'll be moved across country far from you again," Captain asked, but Blaze thought of it more as a rhetorical statement. "Then it's a good thing that Jacqueline has been around to help guide you with the girls."

"Yeah, except she's going to leave at some point and break Tabitha's and Charlotte's hearts. I can't allow that." Blaze watched the yellow and white bubble in the pan.

"And your heart."

Those three words were like tabasco sauce poured down his throat. He removed several plates from the cabinet and broke the eggs up into individual servings. "I'm fine. It's about my girls."

"If you say so, but I've known you awhile now, and Blaze, I've never seen you more excited to leave this place for something outside these walls as I have recently. It's good to have a life outside here."

"You're right. Since my girls arrived, I've been wanting to get home to them more."

Captain chuckled. "So Jacqueline has nothing to do with this newfound love of life outside work?"

"Beyond helping with my girls? No. I mean, we've never even spent time alone. Never been on a date, so I don't see why you're saying any of this."

"Maybe it's time you did see her beyond your girls. Go on a date. Unless you're scared you might discover you actually have feelings for her."

"As I said, she's leaving. There's no reason to ask her out." Blaze plated the eggs and set them on the table. "Come and eat!"

"There's every reason. Because you'll regret it if you don't. You'll never know if Jacqueline Raynor was the one who could have completed you and your family, and once she's gone, it'll be too late to find out. And you never know, she could decide to stay. From what I understand, she never found anything but heartache in New York City, and her friends believe she's been looking for a reason to stay. Maybe you are that reason."

Blaze tried to keep the thought from his head, but the image of Jacqueline asleep with his girls in her arms was the most beautiful sight he'd ever seen. Not only because she was great with Tabitha and Charlotte but because she had depth, a realness about her, and she was solid. Despite all she'd been through, she knew who she was, and he admired that about her. Most women looked for their identity in their relationship. Jacqueline was different. She was strong, independent, beautiful, and like no woman he'd ever known.

Was the captain right? Should he take her out on a real date to see if there was something between them before she left? He wasn't sure he wanted to know, because in the end it wasn't just his girls' hearts he was protecting. It was also his own.

CHAPTER NINETEEN

After two nights of staying with the girls, Jacqueline thought she'd be relieved and ready for Blaze to find a nanny. But instead, she'd found her own home hauntingly quiet. So quiet, she went to the store early and finished assembling Carissa's dress. Even here, though, it was too quiet.

She'd always thought quiet was the perfect solution for creativity and focus, but she'd been more inspired in the last two days than the last two years. She sat down in the center of her shop and spread her designs around her. They were New York worthless, but she was proud of them. They were for teen girls, and they were the first things she'd created without input for years.

The front door opened with a gust of wind, sending her sketches in a whirl around her.

Jackie didn't even try to save them. Instead, she looked up in hopes of finding Blaze and the girls, but to her disappointment, it was Mrs. Strickland and Carissa. The woman who'd been a second mother to her all these years and her only real role model waltzed in on the happily-ever-after air. The one she permanently rode on since marrying Mr. Strickland. It had only taken decades since their first date, not to mention the long-term misery they'd caused each other until they'd finally found their way back together. Relationships were too messy.

Carissa raced around helping gather up the sketches, and Mrs. Strickland retrieved a few that had made it to the front. "Good morning, I hear you've outdone yourself on the wedding gowns, and Carissa said I could come see what you've done so far." She looked to Carissa with the pride of a mother, and Jackie knew there was more to this visit than just dresses. Mrs. Strickland had been the reason the Fabulous Five had been reunited in the first place. She had a way of making things happen.

"What are these?" Carissa exclaimed and dropped to her knees with no poise at all. "They're beautiful."

Mrs. Strickland stood over her, removed her glasses from her purse, and slid them on long enough to study the sketches before removing them again. Jackie respected her bit of vanity and only imagined herself like that at Mrs. Strickland's age. "She's right. Those are something. You should show them to Knox for the show. These are perfect."

"No," she huffed. "Not these. Those designs aren't New York. They're small town."

"I don't think so." Mrs. Strickland stuck one heeled shoe out to the side and mimicked her best runway fashionista look. "I see this plastered all over the world of fashion." Before Jackie could respond again, Mrs. Strickland darted toward the door.

"I thought you wanted to see the wedding dresses."

"Right, well, I tell you what. I have to run to the coffee shop to pick something up from Mary-Beth. I'll be back in a bit. Carissa can wait for me here and go over it with you until I return." She closed the door before either could complain.

"So is this where we're supposed to forever bury the proverbial hatchet?" Jackie looked to Carissa, and they both laughed. Like young school girls, they sat on the floor and giggled as if nothing had ever transpired between them. It was freeing, and for the first time since the dreaded day Jackie had run off with Carissa's fiancé, she truly felt a connection to her friend.

"I missed this." Carissa handed her a few pages. "Do you think you can once and for all forgive me for not seeing the truth behind what happened?"

"The truth?" Jackie asked, scooping the papers to her chest.

"Yes." Carissa scooted closer, knee-to-knee with her on the floor. "That you took Mark away from me to save me from a life of misery."

Tears pricked at the corner of Jackie's eyes. "That was only an excuse."

"No, you still don't see it, do you?" Carissa slipped the pages from her fingers and took both of Jackie's hands. "You're a good person. I wish you would believe us so you'd stop punishing yourself."

Jackie released her dear friend, still unable to completely let herself off the hook for the cruel harm she'd inflicted upon her sweet, innocent Carissa. She pushed to stand and placed her sketches on the table next to the brown bag Stella had left the other day that she'd forgotten about and then ushered Carissa to the dressing room. "It's only the shell of the dress yet to be adorned, but I must see the fit."

Carissa gasped. "It's perfect. Even more beautiful in its simplicity. I know you think I'm a fool, but I really do think the dress is everything I want. Please, let me try it on, and you'll see that I'm right. Just give it a chance."

Jackie slid the dress from the hanger and held it up to Carissa. "You're right. It's you." She stepped out of the dressing room and closed the curtain. "But we still need to fit it."

Jackie retrieved her pin cushion from the shelf and decided to see what was in the brown bag. She peered in and didn't have to open the shoebox to know what was inside, but she did. The over-the-top pink decorated shoes she'd given to Mary-Beth as a joke about how she ran from men after the third date had now been returned to Jackie with a handwritten note that read: *It's your turn. You have to go on a date with the next man who asks you out or wear these shoes to the Sugar Maple dance after the wedding.*

Jackie dropped the note into the bag and eyed the shoes.

"You know she means it. Stella said she'd back her, so my advice is that you accept the next date you're offered."

Jackie turned to Carissa to see her friend in the dress that had been made especially for her. It was flowy, white, with pearl buttons and off the shoulder sleeves. A little taken in at the hips, hemmed, and it would be ready. "You are the prettiest bride I've ever seen."

"Thank you." Carissa lifted the dress above her ankles to walk. "And thank you for being my friend."

Jackie fought for the right words, but expressing her feelings was near impossible. Why did everyone have to talk about their feelings all the time? It was uncomfortable. "Me, too."

There. She'd managed to reciprocate before she grabbed her pins and ushered Carissa to the platform. It didn't take long to hem and pin where she'd need to take in the seams. The door opened. "You're just in time. What do you think?"

"I think you're a talented designer." Blaze's deep voice shattered her focus.

"Ouch!" Carissa squeaked out.

Sorry, she removed the pin and shooed Carissa off the platform. "Go change before you get blood on the material."

Carissa paused at the table. "Now I just need a pair of shoes. The perfect ones that mean something." She eyed the pink running shoes and then slipped into the dressing room.

"She's not wearing those with her wedding dress, is she?" Blaze pointed. "I mean, all I know is not to pair plaid and stripes, and even I know not to wear those things with a wedding dress."

Jackie took a moment to compose herself before she went to stand. When she did, Blaze was at her side, offering her a hand. "Thanks." Her breath was short and forced. Had he come by to see her alone? Maybe she wouldn't have to wear those darn shoes after all. Wait, she didn't want to go on a date with a fireman with kids. Although, he was handsome, kind, and his kids were angels.

"You okay?"

"Yeah, fine, why?"

"You look distracted." Blaze's chest rose and fell before she managed to say anything else.

"I'm fine. Really. Just busy with work, dresses, and parties."

"Right, well, I guess you don't have time to take a break, then."

Maybe she could just go on one date with him, for no other reason than to avoid the shoes. "I can take a break. What did you have in mind?"

"Great. Let's go get a coffee. I didn't sleep well the last couple of nights, and I need a pick-me-up so I can get some work done before I crash."

"Okay, let me ask Carissa if she can watch the shop while we go out for a bit. I mean, for coffee."

"Carissa says yes," she hollered from the dressing room. "I'll watch the shop until you get back."

"Great. I thought we could finish going over the plans for the dance."

Jackie retrieved her purse from behind the desk. She squatted for a moment to hide her disappointment. It wasn't a date. It was a work coffee. "Yeah, about that. The Fabulous Five had a meeting and came up with the idea of combining the school dance with the wedding reception." When she stood, she saw the realization in Carissa's eyes, too. What did it matter? She didn't want a real date with him anyway, only to go out long enough to not lose the new bet.

"That doesn't sound like a bad idea. The girls still get their dance." Blaze nodded his approval.

Jackie took the dress from Carissa and then whispered, "Don't worry. I'll win the bet. Since when can a man resist my charms?"

Carissa didn't release the hanger. "Don't play games. They'll only lead you down the wrong path."

Jackie ignored her warning and took Blaze by the arm with a flirtatious smile. "You don't mind, do you? My heels wobble on the cobblestone."

She winked back at Carissa, who only shook her head, and Jackie realized Carissa was right about one thing. She was playing games. But games could be so fun when played right. And there was no way Blaze would make it through coffee without asking her to dinner.

CHAPTER TWENTY

Maple Grounds was packed full of people, but Blaze managed to squeeze in next to Jacqueline at a table near the window. She'd held his arm the entire way to the coffeehouse, but it didn't have the same effect on him it did before. The way she clung to him and flipped her hair was like watching a bad romantic comedy.

Jacqueline remained standing, looking down at her chair. He pulled it out for her, and she sat with a wave of her hand. "So gentlemanly of you."

Perhaps he'd been mistaken about the woman he'd seen who possessed talent, tenderness guarded by strength, and a depth like no one else he'd met. Now that he thought about it, he'd only seen her that way for a few minutes because he longed for a mother for his girls. Not that he'd even really considered that. He'd planned to raise them on his own. But there had to be something to that, because the Jacqueline by his side was the last woman he'd ever want to date. Actually, she would be the perfect date before his girls had arrived, but the bachelor life was no place to raise kids. He eyed the line but figured it wouldn't take long. "Would you like something?"

She ran a manicured nail down his arm. "Tell Mary-Beth to make something romantic for me."

People watched her flirtations, and he knew it wouldn't take long for the entire town to know. He couldn't hold his question in any longer. "What's going on? You're acting strange."

"Strange? I'm not acting any different than I normally do." Her gaze remained on Mary-Beth working behind the counter filling orders.

He decided standing in line would be more comfortable than staying at the table with Jacqueline. "I'll be back."

The espresso machine steam rose to the ceiling, and the people chatted around him. He checked his phone several times to see if it was time to pick the girls up, or if work had called, or anything to distract him.

"Hey, man. How's it going?" Drew Lancaster joined him in line, smacking him on the back as if they'd known each other their entire lives. He was a good guy, but sometimes he tried too hard to fit in like a local to make Carissa happy. Funny what women made men do.

"Hey, how's it going?" Blaze scooted up a few steps.

Drew waved at Jacqueline, who hadn't taken her eyes off Blaze, making him feel uncomfortable.

"Looks like you and Jacqueline are getting along well. You two becoming a thing?"

Funny how a matter of hours could change a person's perspective. If Drew had asked him that same question last night, he would've had to think on it for a minute. But the independent, confident, yet vulnerable woman had morphed into a needy, clingy person who wouldn't give him breathing room. "No. Not a thing at all."

"Great, Stella was right." He pointed out the front window to Knox and Stella on the front walk.

"Right about what?" Before Drew answered, they reached the front of the line.

"Hey, Blaze. What can I get you?" Mary-Beth spoke in a quick clip, obviously trying to get through the rush of people who had come in for their morning caffeine hit.

"I'll take a coffee, black. And Jacqueline will have—" he swallowed and leaned over the counter to speak as soft as possible "—something romantic. She said you'd know what she would want."

Mary-Beth burst into laughter. "Is this a date?"

"No. Not a date," he announced a little louder than he'd intended.

Mary-Beth and Drew both snickered, as if they were in on a big joke Blaze didn't hear. He looked between them both and at Jacqueline, but he couldn't see her through the crowd. "Why do I feel like I'm the punch line?"

Mary-Beth didn't answer but went to work on the drinks while Serena rang up his coffee. Blaze stood nearby until Drew completed his order.

The moment the transaction finished, Blaze swooped in for the attack. "Okay, spill it. What's so funny?"

"Jacqueline's production."

"I don't get it." Blaze ran a hand through his hair.

Mary-Beth slid two cups onto the pick-up counter. One of them was pink. "Tell her those shoes are going to look darling with her dress at the Sugar Maple Reception Dance."

He caught on quick. "Okay, so there's obviously a Fabulous Five bet going on and I'm in the middle of it. I can't believe you girls still do that. Didn't you outgrow it after high school?"

Drew smacked him on the back again. "You *are* the bet."

Mary-Beth tapped the cup. "He's not too far off. The bet I made last fall was that I'd have to wear a pair of outrageous pink and bedazzled tennis shoes if I canceled before the third date with Seth. Well, I did because I fell in love with Tanner. Which meant I had to wear those darn shoes to Mr. and Mrs. Strickland's wedding. The other day I sent the shoes to her with a bet she wouldn't even go out on one date, and if she doesn't, she'll have to wear the shoes to the reception dance."

Blaze didn't know if he was angry or relieved that there was an explanation for Jacqueline's quick behavior turnaround. "Listen, can you both do me a favor?"

They shrugged.

"Don't tell Jacqueline that I know. I'd like to give her a little payback for me being the object of the bet."

Mary-Beth raced away to make the next beverage with a quick thumbs-up.

Drew shook his head. "Be careful. You don't have a clue about the woman you're playing with. She's been known to explode when someone has done her wrong."

"Don't worry… I put out fires for a living." He took both cups and strutted across the coffee shop to settle next to Jacqueline. "Here. I think you'll enjoy this, but if not, I'm sure I can find something even more romantic to do." He tucked her hair behind her ear and slid his lips down her jawline. "Something much, much more romantic."

She stiffened, but he didn't hold back. Instead, making sure his lips grazed her earlobe, he whispered, "Why don't we find someplace quieter for just the two of us?"

Before she could respond, he eyed the crowd, who undoubtedly saw the faux intimacy between them. He took her hand and kissed each knuckle. "I have all day before the girls are out of school. You know, now that you have made friends with my girls, there's nothing holding me back from telling you how I feel about you. Jacqueline, you're beautiful, talented, and sexy. You drive me crazy, the way you try not to bite your lip, but you can't help it when no one is looking. The way you glide through a room like an angel."

Jacqueline jolted away, grasping at her coffee cup like it was her life raft. She eyed the pink cup and him. "No, not worth it. Don't care."

"What?" Blaze acted as if he had no clue what she was talking about.

"Nothing. I've got to go. Sorry."

"I thought we were going to talk about the school dance and wedding reception being combined?"

"I'll take care of it. I'll take care of everything." She bolted from the coffee shop like a cat from a burning building.

It was fun to watch Jacqueline squirm, and he wanted to keep it going, but there was work to be done and he didn't have much time, so he chased after her. For a woman in heels, she moved fast. "Wait."

"I have to get back to the store." She rushed ahead, but he caught her by the time she reached the corner.

He grabbed hold of her arm and spun her around, knocking her off balance, and she fell into his arms. She fought to break free, but she only slid more. "Relax. I know."

She went limp in his arms. "Know what?"

"Everything. The bet. You using me to win it."

Her eyes shot wide. "Listen. I didn't mean to."

"Yes, you did." Blaze stood her upright but didn't let her go. "So there's no reason to hold a grudge on this one. You got as good as you gave." He leaned in, making sure his lips brushed her earlobe once more, and she squirmed. "Desperate isn't a good look for you, by the way."

"Desperate?"

He released her and strutted ahead.

"Desperate? Are you mad? As if I'd ever be interested in a self-centered civil servant who only knows not to put plaid with stripes. I would never be interested in you. Nothing you did could possibly change my mind."

"Really?" He took that as a personal challenge. "So you don't think I could ever get your attention or stir you up inside in such a way you'd long to win me over?"

"Never." She reached the steps to the back door of her store and blocked his path. "Not ever."

He didn't know if it was the personal challenge or the way she looked sexy when she was mad, but either way, it was on. With one arm, he swooped her against him and claimed her lips in a kiss that turned the air electric around them. She tasted sweet, felt euphoric against him. She hesitated, but when she let go, the passion that she'd stored inside escaped and flooded him with heat. And in that one kiss, he realized that he was lost forever in the unattainable white picket fence fantasy he never wanted, with a woman who was all wrong for him and his girls and would be gone before he could recover from this one kiss.

CHAPTER TWENTY-ONE

Jackie clung to Blaze's tan, strong arms while standing on her shop's back porch. That's where she thought she was, but she wasn't positive because the world continued to spin. Yet, it was as if nothing moved or made a sound around them. No birds chirped, no cars passed, no courthouse clock chimed. All she heard was a pounding in her ears. She wobbled, but he propped her against the banister and strutted away.

She blinked, watching Blaze hop into his truck and drive off. Part of her wanted to scream for him to come back, to hold her and never let her go. Because in that moment when they were touching, everything in life made sense. Once his truck was out of sight, she managed to retrieve her shoes from the steps, where they'd fallen from her feet during the life-altering, toe-curling, oh-my-God kiss. A kiss that erased all other kisses from her mind. A kiss that melted her heart, her body, and her will to run from a man who was all wrong for her. Blaze had wiped every thought of her planned future from her head with that one kiss.

As if zombified from some mind-numbing dissociative disease transmitted from Blaze's warm, soft, strong lips to her now liquified mind, she stood motionless. After a minute, she somehow managed to open the back door and fluttered inside as if she didn't feel the ground beneath her.

Carissa rushed to her side, offering her an arm to keep her from tumbling over. "Are you okay? What's wrong?"

"Drive-by kiss," she mumbled more than spoke before she realized what she'd said.

"Blaze?" Carissa shouted her question but didn't wait for an answer. "And based on the expression on your face, you've been knocked silly."

"Silly? No. I think I was just kissed stupid." She collapsed onto the platform, touching her bottom lip and remembering the heat and the pressure of Blaze's attention.

Carissa cuddled in beside her, unfurled Jackie's fingers from her shoes, and tossed the heels to the floor. "What are you going to do? I've never seen you in such a state."

"What am I going to do?" She laughed—not just any laugh, but the kind that had been trapped inside her since she was taught to be silent while her mother worked when she was four, the jaw-aching, bent-over, unladylike cackle of past sins and forgotten dreams all mashed together at once.

"Are you okay?" Carissa leaned away as if worried she'd catch whatever disease riddled Jackie's body. "I've never seen you like this. Ever."

She fought for breath and sanity. "You're worried about me?"

"Yes," Carissa said.

She shook her head but couldn't stop laughing. Between gasps, Jackie managed to say, "Me, the girl who hurt you." She held her stomach and bent over, trying to regain control of herself.

"It's finally happened… You've broken yourself from guilt, or Blaze broke you with that kiss." Carissa reached for her phone, sobering Jackie from her sky-high release of pent-up emotions.

"Don't you dare call the girls. I'll never forgive you if you even tell them about that kiss. Or my reaction to said kiss." Jackie snatched Carissa's cell and tossed it onto a nearby chair. "Just give me a minute. I need to think." She shot up and paced the floor. "I-I was just caught off guard, that's all. Yeah, that's it."

Carissa sat with her lips pressed together until she blurted, "Are you going to let Blaze know how you feel? He's a great guy. His girls are great. And he obviously likes you. He would be so good for you."

"Good for me? We have nothing in common." She paced faster in her bare feet, hoping she'd picked up all the straight pins from her last fitting. "He's work boots; I'm designer heels. He's a father; I'm married to my work. He's high-spirited; I'm high fashion. Besides, I'm not going to stay in Sugar Maple for a guy. Never going to happen. I have big dreams and big plans."

Carissa remained sitting calmly as if Jackie's entire world wasn't collapsing around her. "When are you going to be honest with yourself?"

"What are you talking about?" She collapsed on the platform where she'd bolted from a breath ago.

"I'm talking about the fact that nothing can stop you when you want something. Not anything or anyone," Carissa said. "It's been a year. If you want New York City so badly, why are you still here?"

Jackie eyed the two teen dresses she'd made for the girls and realized she'd done everything but runway fashion the last few weeks. "You know why. I was run out of New York, shamed from the fashion world."

"That wouldn't stop you. Not if you really wanted to return."

Jackie hated it when her friends were right. "Then I'd better get back to it. No more distractions. I had my fun designing for little girls. Now I need to do some real work."

"If that's all you need to do, why haven't you been doing that?"

"I told you that I had some sort of mental block. I lost my muse."

Carissa stood, pointed to the dresses, and crossed the room. "Doesn't look like it to me."

"You're insane. Those aren't real fashion. They're kids' clothes."

Carissa grabbed her purse from behind the register. "They look designer to me. You need to think about what you really want. I remember when we were young, you dreamed about being married to a dashing hero and that you'd be a mother who would spend time with her children."

"We were kids." Jackie shot up from the platform, slipped her feet into her heels, and grabbed her sketchbook. "You're right about one thing, though. I've been wasting too much time avoiding my goals. Now's as good a time as any to focus." She sat down and eyed the blank page for several seconds, but inspiration floundered and fell to oblivion.

"Right. Well, I'll let you get to work." Carissa darted out the back door, leaving Jackie to face her lack of…talent. Benjamin Langford's words still haunted her. He'd been wrong. The man had stolen her designs and then told the world they were his. When she tried to reveal the truth, he made her out to be an insane, needy, wannabe designer he'd grown tired of. No one seemed to think about the fact she was wife number three. She tossed the pencil. It bounced and flew across the room. The aroma of fresh fabric and failure loomed around her.

She needed to relax and let the creativity flow, so she placed her head in her hands and closed her eyes to see the beautiful creations stuck in her deep mind. Stark blue silk with sparkles like stars flowed through her vision. It shimmered, and she pulled her focus back to see more. And she did. It wasn't fabric at all. It was the blue of Blaze Warren's eyes.

Searing. Stunning. Sublime.

CHAPTER TWENTY-TWO

Blaze sat outside in the elementary school carpool pick-up line waiting for Charlotte, but his mind was elsewhere. If he were being honest with himself, it was still on Jacqueline's soft, plump lips. He'd never thought his body would explode with want with one kiss.

His play had backfired on him, and instead of him teasing her, he was the one left wanting more. A raging need to see her again shredded his resolve to prove to himself Jacqueline was the last woman he'd ever want in his life.

Charlotte bounded down the sidewalk with her bright-golden hair bouncing. She climbed up into the back seat of the truck with an ear-to-ear smile that warmed his heart. He tucked her in with the seat belt snug and headed to the high school. "Have a good day?"

She nodded. He wanted to get her to tell him with words, but at that moment, his focus slipped back to Jacqueline instead of his troubles with his youngest daughter. Somehow he believed that Charlotte would be okay. As a matter of fact, he felt like the world was in a better state since he'd connected with Jacqueline. It was as if he had drunk a mood-enhancing potion. Maybe she was a witch like in the book he read to Charlotte, because Jackie sure had cast a spell on him. Not that he believed in such nonsense.

When he caught sight of Tabitha, he thought he'd gone mad because she looked happy, too. An unnervingly sweet expression lightened her usually sour disposition.

"Hey, Dad." Tabitha joined her sister. "We're headed to the shop, right? Our dresses should be ready."

"Sure," he said way too quickly. "I mean, I have the afternoon off, so yeah."

Tabitha looked at Charlotte, and they both giggled.

"What?" He steered onto the main road and headed to downtown.

"You like Jacqueline," Tabitha said in a sing-song voice.

"What?" He gripped the steering wheel tight at ten and two. "Well, sure. We're friends."

"Friends, huh?" The little girl giggles started again. "How did your friend meeting go with Jacqueline about the dance?"

He drove off the pavement and overcorrected. "Sorry, girls."

"O-M-G. Admit you like her." Tabitha turned sideways, smiled at Charlotte in the back seat then eyed him.

"Don't be ridiculous. All I care about right now is you and Charlotte. Besides, you girls need to remember that she'll be leaving. I don't want the two of you getting hurt again."

Charlotte tapped him on the shoulder and whipped her head back and forth, thrashing her face with her hair.

"You mean *you* don't want to get hurt. Listen. We know love can be tricky and painful, but it's worth it if it works out. You can't give up. You should hook up with her."

"Hook up?" It took all his concentration to turn into the square without hitting any pedestrians. "What are they teaching you at that high school?"

"You can deny it if you want, but how did your meeting go today? Did she lean in while you were talking? Did you hold hands? Susan Peterson says that if someone likes you, they'll lean into you to let you know."

"I'm not in high school." He tried to scramble for words about their non-meeting that was thwarted by teasing, playing games, and a kiss that sent him running. "Um, yeah, about the dance, I'll let Jacqueline fill you in on the details."

He pulled into the back lot and shoved it into Park, relieved that he was able to concentrate enough to get his girls here safely.

"I hope my dress is ready," Tabitha said with the enthusiasm that only could flow from a teenage girl.

"I guess we'll find out." His breath hitched, and he felt like he was a teenager himself about to take a girl to the school dance.

"Come on." Tabitha opened the door and hopped down, followed by Charlotte, but he couldn't move. "Dad!"

"Go ahead. I'll be right there." He waited for the girls to race into the shop, and then he rested his head against the steering wheel. How had he gotten himself into such a messed-up situation? He'd wanted to be a good father. Jacqueline said herself that she'd never make a good mother. And she'd be gone soon. She'd made her intentions clear, and he needed to protect his daughters, not chase after empty dreams of a real happily ever after instead of a forced marriage from a pregnancy lie. He'd spent six years trying to make that last relationship work. Work was the key term. It was exhausting, and he'd had every reason to stay together for the kids, but in the end it fell apart. Had it ever been together, though?

He entered the shop and found the girls giggling in the dressing room and Jacqueline standing in her tall shoes, long legs, and enchanting smile.

She was a vision. "Hey there."

"Hey," she said, sauntering over. Her perfume surrounded him in a sensual rosy scent.

"Do girls ever stop giggling?" he asked, glancing back at the dressing room.

"Not until they lose their innocence, so enjoy it while you can."

"That's a chilling thought." He studied the curve of the toe of his boot.

She touched his wrist, sending a jolt through him, but she backed away before he could fully register the gesture. "Listen, we should talk."

"Not here, not now." He eyed the little feet showing beneath the curtain. "Tonight after the girls are in bed."

She nodded before the curtain flew open and out stepped his daughters in darling dresses. Charlotte indeed looked like a princess, with all her blonde curls and the pretty pale blue and silver dress. Tabitha, though, looked beautiful and not at all like the little girl she no longer was. But Jacqueline had told the truth.

"You were right. It is appropriate for her age," he told Jacqueline. He walked over and kissed his girls on their heads. "You both are the most stunning young ladies ever."

"Oh, Dad." Tabitha had tears in her eyes, and in that moment, he knew how to connect with his eldest daughter. An open heart with nothing but love to offer instead of judgement. He looked to Charlotte, but she remained a mystery. As did the redhaired goddess who'd put such smiles on their sweet faces. How could she believe that she'd be a horrible mother, when she'd brought his girls out of their shells with such ease? A task he'd failed to do on his own.

"You did an amazing job," Blaze said to her as he hugged his daughters to him. "You really are talented."

"Please… What do you know about fashion?" She fluffed Charlotte's princess skirt.

"Maybe nothing, but I know that I've never seen dresses like these before. They're original and as if you created them with their individual personalities in mind. I think you've got something special."

"I agree." Tabitha twirled in front of a three-way mirror. "All the girls are going to be so envious at the dance."

"Dance. Right. We need to get to work. I needed to tell you girls that Carissa and Stella have offered to open up their wedding reception and combine it with the school dance. Since it was set for the same night, it should work out well. This means the Knox Brevard show will also be filming, so you can show off your dresses on the show." Jacqueline grabbed her laptop and settled in at the table.

"That's an awesome idea!" Tabitha had stars in her eyes, clearly excited about the idea of being on the show.

Charlotte pointed at herself.

"That's right. You'll be there too since it is part of the wedding reception." Jackie unhooked the top of Charlotte's dress for her. "Why don't you girls go take off your dresses and hang them up? I'll put them in garment bags for you to take with you. Also, I'll help you pick out the right shoes later, too."

She shooed them to change while she grabbed a box and folder. He was in awe over how much work she was willing to put in for two little girls she barely knew instead of focusing on her own business or her escape from small-town life. Maybe she really *didn't* want to leave and she *was* looking for an excuse to stay.

"Thanks again." He swallowed a lump that had been lodged there all afternoon. "You're really good with children."

"No." She chuckled. "I'm good with fashion and the girls like fashion, that's all. It has little to do with me."

Before he could argue, the girls darted out, and they all sat around the glass table.

Jacqueline opened her notebook to one of her lists. "So we have supplies for decorations, food is taken care of since the town is contributing with the wedding reception, and the dresses are done. But we still need to get volunteers to run the dance and venue since the reception staff will be busy with the food distribution."

"You and Dad can chaperone," Tabitha said, her words filling Blaze with such pride. "I mean, if you don't mind."

Jacqueline shot him a stay-cool look, so he took a breath to steady himself and said, "Sure. I'd be happy to if it helps."

Charlotte pointed at her chest with her thumb.

"Don't worry. I'm sure we can find someone to stay with you for the evening. I bet Mary-Beth will volunteer," Jacqueline said with a wink. She handed out some dry flowers, ribbons, and other decorations. "Let's work on the centerpieces first."

He attempted to help, but he was all big fireman hands that didn't tie little bows well. Not to mention the distraction each time he caught Jacqueline glancing at him. She leaned into him and took both his hands in hers, stealing his breath. "Here, like this."

"I told you so," Tabitha said under her breath when he glanced over. Her mischievous grin looked like Cupid had painted it on her face.

They worked all afternoon with a few clients interrupting on occasion to purchase or browse the merchandise. Before he knew it, the clock struck six and it was closing time. "Hey, why don't we finish this up at our house? I'll order pizza, and we can work on those decorations."

"That sounds like a good idea. I'm starving." Jacqueline rubbed her nonexistent belly and turned the sign around. "I'll meet you at your house. And I'll bring your dresses with me."

Tabitha and Charlotte cleaned up without being asked and bolted to the truck.

Blaze stood around like a lost hamster in a maze of emotions. "Can I help with anything before I go?"

"You can order that pizza. I'm going to change, and then I'll be there in about fifteen minutes."

He took the hint and drove the girls to the house, where he

ordered pizza and quickly picked up the mess and attempted to clean the dishes. It was the longest twenty minutes of his life before the doorbell rang, and he raced to answer it, but it wasn't Jacqueline. It was the pizza guy. In that moment, he realized how much he'd wanted it to be Jacqueline, and he knew he couldn't let her go without figuring out if what he felt was real. If caring for someone could be this easy with no bitterness or resentment.

He closed the door and set the pizza on the kitchen table, where the girls rushed with their plates in hand.

"Are you going to tell her now?" Tabitha asked.

"Tell who what?"

Tabitha slapped a gooey piece of pizza onto her plate and licked her fingers clean. "Jacqueline that you love her."

CHAPTER TWENTY-THREE

Jackie snuggled in with the girls and read *Little Women* aloud in Charlotte's bed. It wasn't a shock that Tabitha joined them, snuggling up into Jackie's other side. How many times as a little girl had she dreamed of spending time with her mother like this? Of course, that wouldn't have fit into her mother's schedule and there wasn't time to be needy.

When she reached the end of the chapter, she closed the book. Charlotte tugged on Jackie's sleeve, looking up at her with big blue eyes. "Sorry, but that's it for tonight. I'll read more to you tomorrow."

Tabitha sprang out of bed. "Did you hear that? She's going to come back tomorrow night."

Before Jackie could correct her words, it was too late. There was no way she could squash their enthusiasm. Besides, if she were being honest with herself, she enjoyed those girls so much. It was as if they filled a hole in her heart that had been dug in her own childhood.

She kissed Charlotte on the forehead and tucked her in snug and then turned to find Blaze watching her. Had she done it right? The girls hadn't complained when she'd watched them, but tonight it was different. Blaze was here. Maybe she was supposed to offer her a stuffed animal or something. "I just finished reading." She swished past him and went to Tabitha's room, where she walked over to the bed but didn't dare kiss Tabitha, thinking she was too old for that. "Good night."

"Wait." Tabitha grabbed her hand. "Can I ask you a question?"

"Sure." Jackie sat next to her on the bed.

Tabitha glanced at the door and then sat up and whispered, "You have to promise not to tell Dad."

"I can only promise I won't tell him if it is something he doesn't need to hear. If it's a danger to you or others, then yes I would need to tell him."

"It's nothing like that. I need advice about getting a man's attention."

"Man?" She raised a brow at her.

"He's practically a man since he's a senior."

"Ah, we're talking about Andy Richards."

"Shh. Not so loud." She pressed a finger to her lips and eyed the door once more. "Yes. You see, Avery said that she saw him looking at me in the hall. So Mary said I should talk to him. Sandra said I should invite him to the dance. But Susan said he isn't interested and I'd make a fool out of myself. How do you know?" She took a short breath. "I mean, if he's interested and I don't talk to him or ask him out, what if I miss the chance?"

"The chance?"

"Yeah, the happily ever after chance. The kind that you have with my dad."

"Whoa. No one said anything about a HEA." Jackie shifted on the bed.

Tabitha shrugged. "We can talk about your relationship with my dad later. But just so you know, Charlotte and I approve."

They approved? Why did that cause her chest to warm? She'd

never wanted children or a family. Not one that would interfere with her career.

"Anyway, what do I do?"

Jacqueline forced her mind to stop obsessing over her own male dilemma and focus on the hormonal teenager trying to navigate life without a mother. For now, Jackie was all she had. "I'd say that you should strike up a conversation but casually. More of a 'hey, I hear you've got tons of colleges looking at you for a scholarship. Congratulations."

"And then what?"

"Then you wait. Because this does two things for you. One, you show him who you are. A confident, beyond-your-years kind of girl who doesn't just giggle and point at him. That you're on his level not below it and you don't care about anything but congratulating him. It will put him at ease instead of putting up a shield because a freshman has a crush on him."

"Okay." Tabitha bit her nail. "What's the second thing?"

"Secondly, that conversation will strike up others because men love to talk about their accomplishments. The next time you see him, he'll probably say something like, 'I heard from Penn State, and they're interested, too.'"

"And then I ask him out?"

"No."

Tabitha dropped her hands to her side. "When?"

"You don't." Jacqueline patted her arm. "The key to getting someone like Andy interested is by making it seem like it's his idea to ask you out, not yours. And let's face it. You are a freshman and he's a senior leaving for college, and no matter what you say, you can't change that fact. If you like him that much, you'll still like him in a couple of years. This way, you set up a communication and you foster that relationship until he's ready to see you as a person old enough to date."

"That long?"

Jackie smiled. "All good things come to those who wait. That's what Mrs. Strickland told me long ago."

"And you believe that?" Tabitha asked with an eye roll.

"No, I believe that all good things come to those with a long game plan. If you rush in and try to force something too soon, it'll damage it forever. Besides, would you rather be hanging out with him as a friend, flirting and getting his attention, or be at arm's length because he doesn't want to encourage you when he's leaving?"

"Is that what you're doing?" Tabitha asked with unsettling honesty.

"What do you mean?"

"Are you keeping my dad and us at arm's length because you know you're leaving?"

"No—I mean...well, that's complicated."

"I'm only a teenager and I know you shouldn't do that. Because now is the time. You should know what is here before you run back to New York City. You never know... You might find something worth staying for, but if you never try, you can only have regrets."

"Wait. You don't need my advice. You're already too smart," Jackie teased, and before she thought better of it, she kissed Tabitha on the head and walked out of the room, straight into Blaze's chest.

He took a step back and studied her face. His eyes were serious and heated, and he was looking at her like no one ever had. "She has a point, you know. I think we should discuss it over a cup of coffee. I'll be right out after I tell Tabitha good night."

Jackie made her way to the kitchen and hunched over the counter, fighting for an easy breath. But it wasn't easy. Nothing was easy, not when it came to affairs of the heart.

At the sound of Blaze's footsteps, she straightened, filled the coffee pot with water, and then poured it into the reservoir.

Blaze handled the grounds and turned the machine on while they stood and stared at the dripping brown liquid.

"Listen, you were amazing with the girls in there. You know that, right?"

"Me? I probably did everything wrong. That's why I can't keep being their nanny. I mean, what if I made a mistake and messed those two girls up? What if I mess up and cause you and the girls harm?"

He moved in close, too close, so she grabbed two mugs after searching several cabinets and set them in front of the machine.

"You won't. Why do you think so little of yourself?"

"I don't. I think highly of myself. Ask anyone. I'm stuck up, rude, and always stirring up trouble."

He took both of her hands in his and held them tight. "Listen to me. Despite all your rantings about how you're a bad person, I see you as a beautiful, caring, talented young woman who has so much to offer the world. Why do you want to keep everyone so far from you? I mean, I know about your ex-husband and what happened, but I'm not him. Just like you're not Angela, who tricked me into marrying her, convinced me to give up everything that mattered to me, and then only knew cruelty. I never made her happy. You're easy to be around. I feel a joy when I'm close to you that I never felt in all the years I was with Angela."

"She tricked you?" Jacqueline asked. Her stomach rolled and twisted at his words.

Blaze moved from her and poured two cups, taking his comfort away. She didn't like it. She didn't like the fact that he'd moved away, and she didn't like the fact that she wanted him back.

"Yes, she told me she was pregnant and that we needed to get married. I left med school so I could afford to take care of her and the baby. We had a quick wedding, and then she claimed she lost the baby. I tried to console her, but she said I only married her because she was in trouble and that I never loved her and that

I was mean and cruel, but another baby would bond us, so we had Tabitha. It wasn't until we were in the hospital for Charlotte's delivery and I heard the doctor say that she'd had two pregnancies and two successful deliveries that I realized the truth. When I questioned her about it, she told me it was so long ago, how could she remember? After that, she became even more difficult. The postpartum depression kept her bedridden, and I took care of the girls. It wasn't until I discovered her affair that I finally told her we would make the marriage work or we were done. She said she was done and left, but at that point she told me I'd never see my girls again. It was awful and brutal and messy. Then she moved far away so visitation became difficult." He heaved a sigh through the emotion, and Jacqueline couldn't help herself. She wrapped her arms around Blaze and held him tight.

"I'm so sorry. That's an awful thing to put anyone through."

He held tight to her and whispered, "See, you're not this awful person who fails at relationships because there's something wrong with you. You just haven't found the right person."

"I'm pretty sure I'm the one who's created my mess."

He leaned back, keeping her only inches from his face. "Then that means I deserved what happened to me."

"No. of course not." She caressed his stubbled cheeks. "But that's different."

"How? I was manipulated into marrying a woman over a false pregnancy, and you were manipulated into marry a man so he could steal your designs."

She shook her head, but he cupped her cheek and trapped her gaze in his. "You know it's true. You're just scared. And I don't blame you. I'm scared too. Jacqueline, you've been through enough to cause anyone to shy away from a relationship, but you deserve so much more."

She blinked, attempting to hide her tears. "Jackie."

"What?" Blaze asked.

"Call me Jackie. Jacqueline is like a stage name to me. I use it to keep people at a distance. Only the people closest to me are allowed to call me Jackie." She couldn't hold back any longer because for the first time in years, she wanted to leave the pain behind and embrace future possibilities. She stood on her toes and pressed her lips to Blaze's, where she was lost in her happily ever after chance.

CHAPTER TWENTY-FOUR

For two long days and excruciating nights, Blaze had to work, but he snuck away every evening to visit his girls. Thank goodness his home was only minutes from the station, because every chance he had, they'd stop the truck out front long enough for him to run inside to check on things and to steal another delicious kiss from Jackie. He didn't even care the men razzed him each time.

Finally on day three, he left the firehouse with extra energy and headed straight for the old building they were using for the dance and wedding reception. The poor old structure in downtown couldn't decide what it wanted to be. After it had been abandoned years ago, it had been used as a senior recreation center and now served as a rental venue. It would be drafty and old, so he wasn't sure how a few decorations could make it look like a dance hall, but if anyone could transform the place, it was Jackie.

He stepped onto the creaky wood floor and turned the corner into the main room that sparkled with silver ribbons, streamers, tables, chairs, and crisp white linens. "I don't think you need my help at all."

Jackie shone brighter than anything else in the party space. "Yes, we do. Over there, we need you to assemble the wooden picture booth in the shape of a carriage."

"A carriage?"

"Yes, like the one Cinderella rode to the ball in. Royal theme, remember?" Jacqueline teased.

He crossed the room to be closer to Jackie. "I should have known." He kissed her cheek, and they stood a foot apart in front of everyone as if they still didn't want the world to know how they felt about each other. "How did the girls do last night?"

"Good. Except Charlotte woke up scared. I think she had a nightmare about you stuck in a fire. Tabitha told me this morning when I dropped them at school that Charlotte's been stressed about your job. She says you're going to get trapped in a burning building." Jackie's voice cracked, so he wrapped his arms around her and hugged her tight.

"That won't happen." He stole a quick kiss before Charlotte smacked herself in the forehead and shook her head, but Tabitha snagged both their hands and led them to the white wood sitting in a pile waiting to be assembled. "You two work over here. The rest of us will be over on the other side of the room. Oh, and Mary-Beth said that she can watch us if you have plans tonight." She took off before he could answer.

"Sounds like my girls are playing matchmaker."

"You have no idea." Jackie tucked her hair behind her ear in that seductive way that drove him insane. "They've already started making plans for a family vacation."

"Really?" Blaze held his breath. "And what do you think about that? I mean, I know it's way too soon for anything like that, don't get me wrong, but did the thought of it make you want to run to New York City?"

"Yes," Jackie said as if speaking about the weather and not his crumbling heart. "Because I think Tabitha would love the fashion and Charlotte would love the architecture."

He smiled as if he'd seen his first sunset in life. "Good point."

"What about you? What do you want, Blaze?" Jackie asked.

"I want my girls and you to be happy."

"No, for you." Jackie lifted a hammer and looked at it like it might sprout fangs and bite her. "You wanted medical school, and you settled with being a firefighter. Everything you've done has been for someone else. It's not too late. You could return to college."

He took the hammer from her and sat holding on to her. "No. I don't have that many years to study in me. Not now. Sure, I'm not old, but I've realized I don't have the passion for it, and I wouldn't want to be so distracted for so long and miss the years I have left with my girls. Besides, needles, remember?" he whispered.

"The girls are great, so I understand wanting to be with them." She glanced at them the way a woman would look at her own children. "But what then? I can tell you don't enjoy being away from them for days at a time, but you don't want medical school. There has to be another option."

He turned his attention to building the carriage before it got too late and he wouldn't get any alone time with Jackie after the girls were in bed. "I've thought about becoming a paramedic and switching to a private company. I'm already an EMT, so I only need to complete the paramedic training. It's not as dangerous, and I can work twelve-hour shifts instead of forty-eight. It still has the element of adrenaline that I like but without the risk. I think Charlotte would sleep better, too."

"You should, then. I'm sure you can work something out for training around the girls' schedules."

He put together the base of the carriage and then moved on to the main section. "I'll think about it. Still have to deal with needles, though," he joked.

She slipped in front of him and took the hammer from his hand this time. "If you want it, I'll help with the girls."

"You don't even know how much longer you'll be here." He eyed the carriage because he couldn't look at Jackie and see her face when she told him that it would be days or weeks or months, because none of that would work for him. Not even years would be a blessing if she'd eventually leave.

"I don't know if I'm still leaving." She eyed the girls over her shoulder. "A wise woman once told me that I might just find a good reason to stay."

Her cell phone rang, calling her from his side. It didn't matter, though. Not if she wasn't going to be leaving. His heart floated up in his chest, feeling light and full for the first time in decades.

"Why are you calling me?" Jackie said in a hushed, stressed tone. He was at her side in an instant. "I don't know what you're talking about, and I'm not interested in listening to any of your grand schemes. Besides, I'm a nobody, untalented, hack of a designer that you graced with your name for a short time." She hit the End button, but her hands shook.

"Who was that?" Blaze wanted to reach through the phone and strangle whoever harmed her with their words.

"My ex-husband." She looked distant, wounded, and he only hoped this wouldn't put her walls up again, sealing him out of her life.

"What did he want?"

"My designs." She shook her head. "I don't have any designs, and even if I did, I would never trust him to reignite my career. I can't believe he thought I would be interested in anything he wanted."

"Then you can finally say you're done with him. You don't care about returning and showing him that you're more than he said you'd be. Jackie, you've done it. You've moved beyond all of your past, and you look like you're ready for a future." Blaze waited for her response, and he hoped he hadn't pushed too hard, but he was so proud of her.

"I guess I am."

He wanted to tell Jackie that he was falling for her, that she was everything he could ever want in a woman. Not here, though. "Tomorrow night, do you think Mary-Beth could watch the girls? I'd like to take you out someplace special, just the two of us."

Jackie glowed as if she'd forgotten all about her ex-husband and his devious plans. "I'd like that."

Stella and Carissa rushed into the room and surrounded Jackie with such excitement that he turned his attention to his work, but he couldn't help but listen.

"Did you see? You're a fashion star. Bigger than before. Everyone wants to know where to get your designs." Stella shoved a phone at Jackie, who gasped.

"I don't understand."

Carissa pointed at the screen. "Knox shared these with the promo material for your show, and look at all these comments. You're trending. Fashion designers from around the world are calling you a genius."

"What? No. These are clothes for teens. They're not designed for high-fashion runway." Jackie laughed, but he saw it, the glint in her eyes that she wanted more. More than Blaze could ever offer her.

CHAPTER TWENTY-FIVE

The store had a rush of people, and Jackie received orders that she'd be working on for months to come. Carissa worked the cash register while Drew manned the bakery, and Mary-Beth helped take orders while Tanner ran the coffee shop. Even Stella worked bagging purchased items and Felicia took the constant phone calls.

By the time the doors closed for a late lunch, Jackie collapsed into a chair and kicked her shoes off. "I never thought I'd say this, but I hate these shoes."

Stella collapsed on the plush chair. "I hate to tell you it isn't just your shoes, because my boots aren't even working for me. But this is great, right?"

Carissa closed the register and sat at the table. "I sent Drew a message and asked if the men could send some lunch our way."

"Good thinking." Felicia sat down next to Jackie. "Before I forget, you have over fifty messages."

"Orders? I'll never be able to fill all these. I've never seen a dress shop so busy before. This is insane. I mean, I'm sure it's just a fluke and this will be done by tomorrow, but still. I'll be busy for months."

"Not just orders. Some fashion bigwigs called."

Jackie bolted upright. "I hope you told my ex I'm not interested in him fixing my designs and selling them under his brand. I'm older, wiser, and meaner now."

Felicia pulled out some handwritten notes. "Good for you, but it wasn't just him. It was names like Wes Graden, Fernando Vici, and Jona Silaki."

Jackie gasped. "No. Seriously? What did they say?"

"There were congratulations, some requests for you to call them back, and some offers of working with them."

"Jona Silaki doesn't work with anyone. He's a legend and doesn't need any low-end designers to make his brand bigger."

Felicia thumbed through the papers and handed her one. "Here's his number. You should call him and find out what his offer is. It's what you've been saying you wanted since you returned to Sugar Maple."

Carissa leaned forward. "That's if you still want to return to New York."

Jackie had decided to stay, had even told Blaze as much, but this was beyond anything she could have imagined. It was everything she'd ever wanted. But it probably wasn't even what Felicia had said. It was at best congratulations to returning to the world of fashion. "I should return his call." Taking the little piece of paper, she went to her office and dialed the number, which was obviously for his secretary.

After one ring, someone answered. "Hello?" It was him. It was Jona Silaki. "Hello?"

"Hi. Um, sorry, this is Jackie…Jacqueline Raynor. I received a message that you called. I apologize for it taking so long to return the message, but my shop has been flooded with people today."

"I'm not surprised," Mr. Silaki said. "Your designs are revolutionary. You've blended high fashion for the younger market. Something that all designers have attempted to do with little success. There are either teen clothes or high fashion. One of the complaints from the customers we work with is that their kids look like they're trying to be adults. More and more teenagers are attending galas, parties, show premiers, business events with their families. They need age-appropriate outfits that are made with high fashion in mind. That's what your designs have done. I would love to fly you to New York to speak with me and a few others in my design company about the possibility of a partnership."

"Partnership?" Jackie wanted to pull the word back into her mouth since she sounded confused and undeserving.

"Yes, Ms. Raynor. I'll email you the details. We'd like to have you come up tomorrow, but you can work out the details with my staff."

"I appreciate the opportunity, sir. I need to figure a few things out first, though."

"You do realize the opportunity I'm offering you."

"Yes, I do." Jackie cleared her throat. "I'll know by the morning."

Mr. Silaki was silent for a moment. "Listen, I didn't like what Langford did to you, and I can assure you this will be a business arrangement with lawyers and contracts. I will never call you a has-been who only made it through my name."

Jackie nodded as if he could see her. "I'll confirm in the morning."

"Great. My secretary will reach out to you and handle the arrangements. Good day. I look forward to working with you."

The phone went dead, and Jackie felt like her heart had, too. She rose and walked barefoot out to the store's main room. "Carissa, can you put a sign out front that says sold out, that I'll reopen in a few days, please?"

"Sure." She stood and retrieved paper from the printer. "What's wrong?"

"Nothing." Jackie thought about confiding in her friends, but not this time. Not with everything at stake. This was a decision she needed to make on her own without influence from the people she cared about who only wanted her to stay in town but could never understand why she wanted to go. A list. She needed to sit down and write out the pros and cons and make a logical decision. Last time she'd jumped at the opportunity and given her heart away. Now she had to choose between family life or success on an epic level.

Stella headed for the door. "Right. Don't forget we have filming in a couple of days, too." She picked up the brown bag that still sat in the corner and tossed it on top of the table. "Don't forget these for the party. That's unless you go on that date tonight with Blaze."

"You know about that?"

"Of course. Mary-Beth is watching the kids for you."

Mary-Beth offered an apologetic smile. "She got it out of me. You know how intimidating she can be."

Felicia took Mary-Beth by the arm. "I'm happy to help. Why don't we meet here to get the girls, and then we can take them to the coffee shop for a while. I know there's a young lady who would like to talk with Andy."

Mary-Beth went out the front door mumbling something about her brother leaving and needing to make sure the girl didn't get hurt.

Stella and Carissa eyed their wedding gowns, still on the mannequins. "Are you going to be able to finish in time? Our weddings are only a couple of weeks away. Can you handle the town dance reception and everything else?" Stella asked.

"Yes, of course. Is there anything I haven't been able to handle?"

"Not to mention it will all be filmed and the film crew will be working with you the rest of that night and the next day so the show can be released next month."

"Got it." Jackie willed Carissa and Stella out of her shop, but it took a couple more minutes until they left and she could get paper, pen, and work on her list. She drew a line down the middle. On the left was "reasons to stay with Blaze and the girls" and on the right "reasons to go after my dream job."

In about fifteen minutes, she'd only managed to scribble three on each side. Launch of career, fame, fortune on one side, and Blaze, the girls, and her friends on the other.

She pushed the list away and rested her head on the table. What could she do? How could she make everyone—including herself—happy? She closed her eyes and must have drifted off to sleep, because the next thing she knew, someone cleared their throat and stood over her. She blinked and rubbed her eyes, sure she'd smeared mascara all over her face.

"You should go." Blaze's deep, wounded voice broke through her fog. She looked up to find him in a suit holding flowers and her list. The list of reasons to go or stay.

She snatched it from him. "I'm so sorry. I must've fallen asleep. Let me run and change, and then we can go."

"No." Blaze dropped the flowers on the table and held out the list. "We need to talk."

And with those words, she knew all their progress had been washed away in one moment.

CHAPTER TWENTY-SIX

Blaze sat at the table fighting against his own instincts to tell Jackie what a huge mistake she was making, but he cared for her too much. "I won't be the reason you give up such opportunities. If your ex-husband is offering you something that you want, you should go after it."

She yanked her chair closer and rested her hands on his knees. "It's not like that. I'd never trust him again. And because of you, I know I'm worth more than games and anger. That's not what that silly list was about. You would win every time if that were all."

She bit her lip.

He captured her hands and never wanted to let her go again. "Then tell me. I want to know what has you torn between New York and here."

"I've received an offer. Something beyond my dreams, and that's what makes this so difficult. Jona Silaki has asked for a meeting about a partnership for my teen line."

"That's amazing, right? You were born to be a major label. We both know that."

She laced her fingers between his. "Yes, but at what cost? I can't live here and work there. But I don't want to leave here."

"You can't pass up such an opportunity. It's been your lifelong dream." His insides twisted, but he knew he couldn't hold her back. "I was forced to give up on my dreams, and I'd never do that to you. Go. There's nothing for you here in Sugar Maple."

"It's just a silly list." Tears escaped down her cheeks, and he felt more for her struggle than for his own grief. That's when he realized he'd fallen in love with her.

He swiped her tears away with his thumb. "No, it's what you do to process. I could pretend that I would consider a long-distance relationship, but you and I both know you'd be far too busy for such an arrangement, and I can't do that to my girls."

"I know." She squeezed his hand so tight, he knew she was struggling with facing the truth.

"Go. At a minimum, take the meeting. I know you'll do the right thing. If the opportunity is a good one, then you'll take it. If not, then you'll return until the next opportunity comes along."

"Blaze," she whispered, but he withdrew from her touch, her beauty, her world, and returned to his own as a small-town single dad firefighter.

"Thank you."

She stood, wobbling, but he didn't reach for her. "For what?"

"For showing me that love is possible even after such pain."

"What about the girls? I should tell them." She bowed her head.

"Don't be ashamed of your choice. And I'll tell them. I'm their father. It's my responsibility." Blaze kissed her on the cheek, savoring the aroma of her floral perfume and the touch of her warm skin, and then he retreated out the door to his truck and drove away, leaving his heart behind.

He pulled around the back of Maple Grounds and collapsed against the steering wheel, heaving deep breaths through the pain. The kind of pain he hadn't felt since the day he'd found out his wife was leaving with his girls in tow. A pain that was indescribable, but he didn't regret it. He'd never regret getting to know the real Jacqueline Raynor.

He took a few minutes to collect himself, but there was no avoiding the inevitable. With his chest aching and tight, he rubbed his sternum while he made the short drive home. The sight of the girls through the window dancing around with Mary-Beth and Tanner watching looked like a family scene in one of those romantic movies. For a second, he'd believed in happiness, but now he needed to focus on the practicalities of life.

The night air brought the smell of fresh flowers and lost hope. He shuffled to the front door and took a moment to collect himself. Despite his own feelings, the girls would need him to be strong. Perhaps if he made it sound less tragic, it wouldn't be such bad news to them. He pushed his shoulders back and entered the house with a forced smile. "Hi."

"What did you forget?" Tabitha rolled her eyes. "He's always forgetting stuff."

Charlotte stopped midspin and looked at him, walked up, and wrapped her arms around his middle and cried.

Tabitha shook her head. "No, you have a date tonight with Ms. Raynor. You shouldn't be here. Go." She pushed him toward the door, but he stood firm.

"If you two don't mind, I need to speak with my daughters alone."

Tabitha stomped off. "You ruin everything!"

Her door slammed, but Charlotte stayed attached to him as if he'd disappear if she let him go. And it was like that all night and even the next morning. His youngest clung to him like a fading dream, and all he could do was hold her tight.

CHAPTER TWENTY-SEVEN

It didn't take long after Blaze left for the Fabulous Five to appear in her shop. Each one with that pitying gaze Jacqueline hated so much.

"You all act like I'm going to the funeral of my career. Haven't you heard? It's been reborn."

Carissa ushered her to the table and sat her down.

Felicia pulled up the chair to Jackie's other side. "It's okay. We know how much this must be tearing you up."

Mary-Beth plopped a Frappuccino that looked like the coffee version of the burrow-your-sorrows-in-ice-cream tub. Jackie slid the straw into the drink and took a long, brain-freezing gulp.

"You've got something good here. My vote's you stay with Blaze."

Jackie didn't have the energy to accuse her of trying to manipulate the situation for the benefit of the Knox Brevard show. Besides, she knew it wasn't true. Stella wouldn't do that.

"I agree." Felicia, the diplomat of the bunch, uncharacteristically pounded her fist once against the table as if she passed judgment on the subject.

Carissa cleared her throat. "No. That would be selfish of all of us. We all know how much Jacqueline has wanted this. I vote she should go."

Mary-Beth toyed with her oversize earrings and opened her mouth and then shut it again.

"What? I know you have an opinion." Jacqueline eyed her over the mound of whip cream now dripping down the side of the plastic lid.

Mary-Beth turned her attention to her bracelets, spinning them faster than a tilt-a-whirl. "I'm with Carissa, but I didn't want to say it aloud because it breaks my heart to say it."

"Great, the Fabulous Five is split down the middle. Thanks, this helped a ton. Really." Jackie removed her heels, unbuttoned her jacket, and headed for the door.

"What are you going to do?" Stella asked.

Jackie sighed. "Take the meeting. It's been my dream forever, and if there is a chance I'm going to give it up for a new one, I better figure out if it's still worth it."

She fell into bed that night and cried herself to sleep. Puffy eyes, stuffy nose, and a broken heart was all she had to show for her special non-date evening.

The next morning, the short flight to New York City felt like days instead of hours. The friendervention of the Fabulous Five committee last night had only left her more confused.

A rush of people flooded around her at the airport, but she had never felt so alone before. She hurried through the waiting area to a man at the bottom of the escalator holding a sign with her name on it. Settled into the back seat, she checked her phone for the fourth time, but still no text from Blaze.

The skyline welcomed her to her city home, so she shoved her phone into her purse and lifted her chin. This was her opportunity, the chance she'd worked for since she'd first started designing. If she had known that the Knox Brevard show and a few children's outfits would land her back in good standing with the fashion world, she would've fought harder to be the first segment. Then she would've never run into Blaze repeatedly at the nursery fire at Felicia's place, or at the Strickland wedding, or coffee shop, or anywhere else. She would've moved back before any of that.

She needed to forget about the temporary distraction that had detoured her plans. Buildings passed in a blur, but she spotted the old highrise she had lived in with Ben near Central Park. When the car turned down the side road leading to the office building, she gripped her purse handle tight and took in a few calming breaths. The adrenaline she'd craved for so long poured through her, and she knew she always did her best work with a bit of stress.

The door opened, and she slid out with the dignity of a princess and sauntered through the large glass doors to the front desk, where a stick-thin model receptionist offered a fluorescent white smile. "Can I help you?"

"I'm Jacqueline Raynor, here to see Jona Silaki."

"Take the elevators to the fourteenth floor, and the doors will open into his offices." She pointed to a hall by her side.

"Thank you."

The woman blinked at her since her southern manners were a culture shock to the young city girl. Jackie didn't bother to explain herself, but she took the time during the elevator ride to remember her New York persona and pasted back together her tough-girl façade that Blaze had chipped away.

The doors slid open, and she waltzed into the reception area with her nose so high, she thought she could touch an angel with it. "I'm here to see Jona Silaki."

"Ms. Raynor, wow, it's so amazing to meet you," the receptionist exclaimed in a thick southern accent that took her off guard. "I saw you on the Knox Brevard show, and well, I grew up in Alabama, so I can relate to the small-town struggles."

Jackie eyed the woman, but she couldn't help but offer a friendly smile and nod.

"Right. Come with me. They're waiting on you." She slid from behind the desk and waved for Jackie to follow.

The office space was more like a museum meets penthouse for Elton John. The gold, white, and turquoise palate spoke of elegant expense. When she'd first arrived in New York, she'd interviewed for a job at Silaki Designs and was sent home before she could even open her portfolio. No one in any fashion house had given her the time of day until she'd made her splash with Benjamin Langford. Then it was more a grudging acceptance.

At the large wooden doors with long handles, Jackie prepared herself for a tough meeting of insults and pressure to convince her to sign over her designs and then she'd be another minion under Silaki.

That wouldn't work for her, not this time. Not after what happened with Ben.

Jona Silaki stood in his all-white suit with two people on each side of him. "Ms. Raynor, welcome. We're so glad you could make the meeting. How was your flight?"

"Fine." She remained ready for the onslaught of insults and comments about her mediocrity as a designer. Sure, he'd been complimentary on the phone, but when the negotiations started, she was sure he'd put her down and make her feel like she needed him to survive the world of fashion.

"Please sit. Can we get you anything? Tea, perhaps? Water?" one of the people at his side dressed in all black asked.

"No, thank you. I'm fine." She swiveled the chair, sat in it, and faced them, plopping her purse and portfolio on the massive table. With her ankles crossed, she watched the others settle in across from her.

"I won't waste your time, Ms. Raynor. As I mentioned, we're interested in your latest line for teens. As you know, I have made a name for myself, and my brand is known all over the world. I believe I can take your designs and make them the most sought-after fashion in a decade."

He was going to take her fashion and produce it under his label. No, she'd already tried that. She'd never do that again. Jackie held up her hand to them. "I appreciate you flying me out here for a meeting, but I'm not willing to sell you my designs and then spend years working for you."

The minions leaned in, and rushed whispers flooded between them.

Silaki shook his head. "I think there's been a misunderstanding, Ms. Raynor."

She pushed from the table, took her purse and portfolio. "Thank you for your time. Anyone else would appreciate the offer to work under your label. I'm sorry I'm not that person."

"Ms. Raynor, you must understand, I can't support another label, but the designs will be yours. We'll let the attorneys work out the details, but I want you to partner with Silaki under the Silaki brand. Your office will be set up on this floor, but you will run it, and yes, you'd be a part of our family. We'll develop the Silaki Couture for Teens label, and you'll run the entire department."

Jackie eyed the five-man team of Silaki Designs and knew she'd only be a sixth at the table, and there was no way she'd ever give up the best man she'd ever known, the children she never knew she wanted who she fell in love with, to sit in the sixth chair of a company. "Mr. Silaki, I truly appreciate your offer, but I am afraid I'm going to have to pass. I've already attempted the New York fashion world the traditional way. But now I realized I've never been a traditional girl. This time, I'm going to do it my way. And that way will keep me in Sugar Maple, Tennessee, where I'll design and manage Just Jackie on my own. I'd rather have a big shop in a small town that I own than be a small person in a big company that I don't."

After they expressed their regrets but shook her hand and

wished her well, Jacqueline left New York and took the first flight home. Not because she didn't think she was good enough to work in New York City but because she felt worthy enough to be loved by Blaze and his girls. But could she convince them she'd be there to stay, or was it too late?

CHAPTER TWENTY-EIGHT

Maple Grounds closed in around Blaze with prying eyes and small-town gossip. Davey shuffled inside with Ms. Hughes on his arm. After he seated her at a bistro table, he came to stand in line with Blaze.

"I can bring your coffee to you," Blaze offered. No one ever made a town elder stand in line.

"What? You think I'm too old to get my own coffee or one for my fiancée?" He wiggled his brows and elbowed Blaze in the side. "Just joshing you. Listen, when you going to fly after that girl of yours and shake some sense into her? She don't belong in New York. She's a Sugar Maple girl."

Blaze shifted between feet and eyed the front register, looking for an escape from the conversation. "She's where she belongs."

"Should tar and southernize you right now for being stupid. Fine, get our coffees. Mary-Beth will know what we want." Davey left, but his mouth kept running on and on about how stubborn and wrong Blaze was for letting a woman like Jackie get away. "Fire's done burned too many brain cells."

Blaze reached the front and found Mary-Beth with a sympathetic gaze.

"Don't you worry. Serena is going to cover the shop for me tonight, and I'll be staying with the girls. We'll have fun watching movies and doing girl stuff, promise."

"Thanks. I've got to get to work. Tell the girls I love them, even if they think I'm evil." He forced his legs to move once more, realizing that moping around the coffee shop and watching Jackie's store like a bad stalker in hopes of spotting her back in town wasn't doing anyone any good.

He reported to work, where the men didn't razz him or make him cook, which was worse than when they had. It only meant they felt sorry for him, and there was nothing worse than that. He ignored them and worked on cleaning the rig until the alarm sounded.

Relieved to have a fire to fight instead of his own demons, he suited up.

"This is it," Marco said before hopping into the rig.

The alarms continued to ring, echoing through the bay.

"Three-alarm fire boys," Captain said through the mic. "It's raging toward town. We'll be first on scene."

Before Blaze could even process the information, they rolled onto the scene with flames already blazing from the roof of the warehouse at the edge of town. Sparks flew toward the neighboring homes, and two were already smoking. They all were suited up, ready to go. Commands were shouted. "This is a class-A fire, boys. Get that hose deployed."

They all scrambled to do what they'd been trained for.

"Charge the hose!"

"Warehouse fully involved. Containment."

They all worked together and attempted to keep the fire from spreading into town. The second rig rolled up and assisted. A screaming woman being held back by police caught Blaze's attention when he stepped from the front line for a break, already feeling the effects of dehydration.

"My son's inside!"

Blaze caught sight of where the woman was looking, a house only two doors from the warehouse. "Don't worry, ma'am. We'll go." He raced over to the captain. "Interior attack. Child inside." He pointed to the structure and then took Marco and David and had another team move in with the hose.

Inside, the dark gray smoke restricted visibility. The heat was intense, and flames licked at the ceiling.

"Fall back. Too hot." David yanked at his jacket, but Blaze wouldn't let a kid die. Not now, not ever. He managed to find his way down the hall, calling out but with no return. At the second room where the flames hadn't taken hold, he heard a whimper. "Come on, kid. Come to me."

Blaze rummaged around until he caught hold of a child and scooped him up in his arms. Exhaustion took hold and he stumbled, but Marco was there to take the child and raced ahead. David helped Blaze from the room. The crackling echoed, boards fell from above, the men retreated, but not fast enough.

The roof collapsed in a fireball all around them.

CHAPTER TWENTY-NINE

Jackie couldn't wait another second to see the girls. She pulled up to town, but it was blocked off. The smell of ash surged through her vents. People mulled about, pointing and clinging to one another. At the sight of Mary-Beth, Jackie abandoned her car and made her way through the crowd. "What's going on?"

Mary-Beth's eyes went wide and her mouth hung open, but she didn't say anything.

Carissa raced over. "Oh, honey. I know he's going to be okay. Don't worry. He's tough."

Jackie searched the area, trying to process what was going on.

Carissa rubbed her arms. "It's Blaze. He's trapped in a fire. They're working it now."

Jackie stumbled back into Stella. Knox caught her and kept her upright. Her head spun with fear and horror, but it settled on the girls and all they'd been through. "I need to go. I have to get to the girls before they hear."

She shot to her car, but it was blocked in.

Stella ushered her to continue. "I'll take you in my Chevy. Come on."

She kicked off her heels and ran up the asphalt, not even feeling the small pebbles digging into her feet. "He has to be okay."

Stella and Knox drove her to the school. The entire time, she thought about the fact she'd give it all up for Blaze to be okay. The job, New York City, fame and fortune, anything and everything to have one more kiss. They pulled up to the high school.

"Get Charlotte and come back to get me here." Jackie bolted from the car, up the steps, and into the front office. "I need to see Tabitha Warren now, please."

"Is it true? Is Daddy dead?" Tabitha cried out from the doorway. "That's what the news is saying. All the kids are listening from their phones."

"No, he's not. Your father's brave and strong, and he'll do whatever it takes to stay with you girls."

"Why? No one else does." Tabitha was angry and lost and confused.

Jackie knew how she felt, and no words could change anything, so she took Tabitha into her arms and held her tight. "I'm taking her home. Sign her out, please." She didn't wait for a response and escorted Tabitha out of the building, where she saw Charlotte waiting for them, big tears rolling down her cheeks.

"This is your fault. You left us. Now Daddy's leaving us." Charlotte raced to Jacqueline and pummeled her little fists at her. "I'm going to be an orphan. I hate you. I hate all of you!" She melted into Jackie and cried and cried.

Jackie rocked her on the front steps of the high school with Tabitha clinging to her side. She wanted to praise Charlotte for speaking, but now wasn't the time. Her words had been musical and tragic all at once. Her heart filled with sorrow and love in a way that was indescribable, even to herself. In that moment, she knew one thing and one thing only: the two girls in her arms meant more to her than fashion world domination. All these years she'd searched for love through success, but now, she'd found the truth. The truth of family and real connections. "No. You won't be an orphan because I'll never let you go again. Ever."

* * *

THEY SAT AROUND HER SHOP, holding on to one another, watching the local news and waiting for word of Blaze and the other trapped men in the home. Jackie held tight to the girls and welcomed her dearest friends into her shop, along with their boyfriends and fiancés and Mrs. and Mr. Strickland. Even Davey and the rest of the elders crowded in to be with them.

"See, girls? No matter what happens, you'll never be alone. You have me and the entire town as your family." Jackie tried to reassure them. "But I know your daddy will be fine." She said the words but heard the hollowness in her voice.

Someone turned up the volume on the television, and the announcer said, "We are live at the scene of the massive warehouse fire that turned tragic today." At the word tragic, both girls tightened their grip on Jackie and she held tight to them. She knew her promises would mean nothing if their mother demanded them back. Jackie had no legal rights to the girls, and in that moment, she prayed like she hadn't prayed in ten years. Not just for her own happiness but for the girls and their uncertain future.

"Tragedy struck when a young mother left her child at home asleep while she ran to the store. Unbeknownst to her, a fire erupted in the warehouse nearby, igniting her home and trapping her child."

Charlotte whimpered.

"Turn it off," Jackie ordered, but before Drew could reach the control, the newscaster continued.

"As for the two firemen trapped inside..."

"Wait," Tabitha yelled and jumped from Jackie's lap, blocking Drew from the remote.

"They have been extracted from the blaze, but their condition is unknown at this time. The child has been rushed to the hospital and is in serious condition but survived thanks to these two selfless men who risked their own lives to save the young boy."

Two pictures flashed up on the screen. The image of Blaze in his firefighter uniform along with one of the other men she'd seen a few times choked Jackie.

The newscaster continued. "These are not firemen. They are Sugar Maple heroes."

Jackie couldn't hold back the tears, no matter how hard she tried. They flooded her cheeks, and she cuddled Charlotte to her chest, holding on to a part of Blaze that remained behind.

The announcer pressed his hand to his ear and then said with a renewed excitement, "This just in. One firefighter who is alive but in serious condition has been rushed to the hospital and will be medevacked from here to the Riverbend burn unit along with the child."

Jackie stood and looked at the girls. The man headed to Riverbend was the one who'd survived, and Blaze was a survivor. "I'm going after your father. I'll make sure he receives the best treatment, and I'll call in every favor I have to bring him home to you." She shot to the door with the girls clinging to her skirt.

"Wait. We want to go too," Tabitha begged.

But how could Jackie expose the girls to such devastation before she knew the entire story? The worst images bombarded her brain of him burned and dying. No. She had to protect his children. She looked to Mrs. Strickland and the rest of her friends and whispered, "Help."

They swooped in with all the right words, and Jackie only hoped that the man being rushed to the hospital was Blaze, because if not, she knew the alternative could be even worse. She choked back the fear and headed for the door, which swung open.

In stepped a dirty, disheveled, exhausted Blaze.

"You're alive?" Jackie couldn't hold back another second. She threw herself into his arms, causing him to fall back against the wall. She kissed him, hard, deep, passionate, showing him how much she had fallen for him and his girls. The only thing that tore her away were Tabitha and Charlotte squealing and crying and wrapping themselves around them.

"It's okay. I have to get back, but a town elder sent a message to the captain about how you were all here standing vigil for me. I had to let you know that I was safe."

"No, Daddy. You can't go back. Never leave me again," Charlotte cried out, and Blaze looked to Jackie with wide, bloodshot eyes.

"She spoke earlier today, and I'd listen to her because I think Charlotte is a wise child." Jackie smiled and cupped Blaze's dirt-stained face. "Don't go."

He squatted down and lifted Charlotte into his arms. "The fire's contained but not out. It's safe now. I won't be entering the building anymore." He kissed Charlotte on the cheek and Tabitha on the head. "But it's good to know you all care so much about me."

Jackie huffed. "Too much, I'd say. I mean, I gave up world fashion domination for you three."

"What?" Blaze's mouth fell open. "I thought it was your big chance."

Jackie looked to her town family and to Tabitha, to Charlotte, and finally to Blaze. "No, I think my big chance is standing right in front of me."

He lowered Charlotte to the ground and took Jackie's hands. "Are you sure? I would never want—"

She pressed a finger to his lips. "I think I'll be more sure if you kiss me."

Blaze swooped her into his arms and claimed her lips with all to see. Jackie knew in that moment, she'd found her happily ever after chance. And she was going to take it.

CHAPTER THIRTY

The town clock chimed the moment Stella and Carissa walked down the aisles. Tabitha on one row and Charlotte on the other, dropping flower petals. Cameras rolled from the sidelines, and everyone in town had crowded into the square for the big event.

Blaze was impressed that Jackie had made their wedding gowns so perfect for them. Stella had some sort of deep V opening in the back with dark sparkles like the reverse of stars in a sky lining the edge of her gown and neckline, while Carissa looked elegant and sophisticated and pure.

He and Jackie had front-row seats to the event and found the view telling. There was no sign of Knox's internet persona, despite the filming. His eyes were only on Stella. Drew fidgeted, but at the sight of Carissa, he simply said, "Wow."

The girls finished at the end and joined Blaze and Jackie at their seats, and they sat back to watch the union of two couples. He was surprised to see even Jackie get choked up at the emotional vows.

The marching band played, the mayor said words, and birdseed was thrown. That wasn't the end of the festivities, though.

Not when Declan got down on one knee at the gazebo after the ceremony and proposed to Felicia in front of the entire town. Once everyone scattered, Blaze held tight to Jackie and led her to the recreation hall for the Sugar Maple Reception Dance. Teenagers flooded into the old building with low lights, glistening candles, and music blaring with songs Blaze had never heard. Apparently he had turned into an old man. His daughters both came, along with half the town. The spring formal turned from high school to small-town event mixed with wedding reception party was the event of the year. That was small-town life, though. And he loved it.

Food crowded the long tables, and even Davey and Ms. Hughes danced…well, swayed together in the corner. Blaze checked his phone again, and to his relief, he'd received the message he'd been waiting for ever since he'd realized being a firefighter wouldn't be conducive to having a wife and children. And he knew in the not-so-distant future, he'd ask Jackie to be his wife.

"Why do you keep looking at your phone? You'll give a girl a complex," Jackie teased. She stood breathtakingly beautiful in her custom dress that had already made the internet trending thingy everyone talked about. She was perfect, from her auburn hair to her pink bejeweled shoes. She'd been a great sport and even told him they wouldn't go on a real date until the wedding reception dance so she could show the girls how committed she was to their friendship.

"I have some news," he announced.

She raised one of her perfectly arched eyebrows at him.

"I wasn't sure I wanted to share it with you until I knew I had a shot, and I'm not sure how I'm going to work out the logistics… or if I even can."

"Tell me, and we can figure it out together."

"I was accepted to Physical Therapy school. It'll take four years, but in the meantime, I've been able to take a position with

EMS as an ambulance driver. The schedule will be flexible. I know it means less time for my girls and you, but I can't continue working as a firefighter."

"I think it's perfect. As for the logistics, you have me now. Neither of us is alone anymore." Jackie took his hand. "Besides, I know since you visited David in the hospital, you've been contemplating a change. I can see you as a therapist. You've been jumping in to help David every chance you've had with his recovery. Besides, you won't have to deal with needles."

"I hope the girls feel the same way. I don't want to miss any more of their growing up. I want to attend every dance, party, play, and school event."

Jackie waved Tabitha and Charlotte over. "Hey girls, your dad has news."

Blaze said, "I want to make sure you guys are okay with this first…" He explained about the possible changes in their lives.

Charlotte leapt into his arms and squeezed tight. "Yes, yes, please, yes. I'll help with dishes, and I'll go to bed without issue while you go to school."

Tabitha looked around the room and then nodded, giving him a small smile. He knew how she felt, even if teenage rep wouldn't let her show it.

"Are you sure, girls? It could mean time away from all of you."

Tabitha shrugged. "No worries. I'll plan the wedding with Jackie."

Before he could say anything to her, a tall, broad-shouldered, way-too-old-for-his-daughter boy came over and tapped her on the shoulder. "Hey, I heard back from University of Tennessee, and it's a full scholarship."

Blaze tensed, but Jackie took his hand and held him back.

"That's fantastic." Tabitha twisted one of her curls around her finger. "You'll have to keep in touch and let me know if you like it there since it's one of the schools I'm considering applying to."

Blaze's muscles shook at the idea of this boy away at college with his girl.

"You want to dance?" The boy pointed to the dance floor.

He eyed his daughter, willing her to say no, but before he could even mention the age difference, they were off with *the boy's* hands on his little girl's shoulders.

Charlotte laughed. "It's okay, Daddy. She knows he's too old for her for now. But she's growing up, and you'll have to let her go sometime." She wiggled out of his arms, and he felt as if his life was about to be upended once more.

Jackie kissed his cheek. "They grow up so fast."

"They do." Blaze watched with apprehension, ready to scoot out onto the floor to separate Tabitha from that boy.

"I have one question before I accept your marriage proposal," Jackie said in a matter-of-fact tone.

That snagged his attention. For a second he thought about telling her he hadn't asked yet, but he saw the tug of her lips into a smile and knew she would always get what she wanted, and it would be his pleasure to give it to her. "What's that?"

"When you're done with school, what do you think about adding to our family? We're still young enough to have more kids. I think I might make a good mother after all."

He pulled Jackie close and whispered in her ear. "I'm ready now. Start planning our wedding."

THE END

RECIPE

Blaze wanted to make a special dinner for Jaqueline for Valentine's day, but with school, work, and two little girls he didn't have much time. That's when he decided to make **Bourbon and Brown Sugar Salmon**.

6 ounces salmon per person
Enough brown sugar to cover each piece
1/4 cup soy sauce
1/4 cup brown sugar (or more to coat the top)
1/4 cup bourbon
1 Tablespoon olive oil

Prepare an oven proof pan with 1 tablespoon oil and place on a burner at medium-high heat. Salt and pepper each Salmon fillet and then place skin side up in the frying pan to brown the top of the salmon. Once browned, flip them so they are skin side down and cover with the soy sauce, bourbon, and then brown sugar. Place in the oven at 350 degrees until internal temperature reaches 135 degrees (cook up to 145 degrees depending on your preference).

Remove and serve with some green beens and roasted potatoes.

READERS GUIDE

1. Jaqueline stole Carissa's fiancé after high school. In her mind, she was doing to save Carissa from a horrible fate with the wrong, cheating man. Do you think you could ever forgive a friend for doing such a horrible thing? Why, or why not?
2. Do you think that Jacqueline returned to Sugar Maple and opened her own shop because she had no other choices, or do you thing she hoped to restore her past friendships?
3. Why do you think that Tabitha and Charlotte fought so hard to bring their dad and Jacqueline together?
4. Do you think Jacqueline was really that anti-relationship, or do you think she'd always wanted to find true love?
5. When Tabitha and Charlotte arrived, do you think that Blaze parented out of guilt or love? Why?
6. Why do you think Blaze never wanted the firemen to know he could cook?
7. Since Blaze did everything he could to make his first marriage work-including giving up medical school-yet

it still failed, how hard do you think it was for Blaze to sacrifice being a fireman for his family?

8. Do you wish that you lived in a town like Sugar Maple? Why, or why not?
9. Throughout the Sugar Maple series we've seen the town elders play a significant role. Do you find that in your community, or has the philosophy that we can learn from our elders disappeared from your local community?
10. Did you strongly dislike Jacqueline throughout the first four books? If so, do you see her in a new light and love her now? If not, why?

ALSO BY CIARA KNIGHT

For a complete list of my books, please visit my website at www.ciaraknight.com. A great way to keep up to date on all releases, sales and prizes subscribe to my Newsletter. I'm extremely sociable, so feel free to chat with me on Facebook, Twitter, or Goodreads.

For your convenience please see my complete title list below, in reading order:

CONTEMPORARY ROMANCE

Winter in Sweetwater County

Spring in Sweetwater County

Summer in Sweetwater County

Fall in Sweetwater County

Christmas in Sweetwater County

Valentines in Sweet-water County

Fourth of July in Sweetwater County

Thanksgiving in Sweetwater County

Grace in Sweetwater County

Faith in Sweetwater County

Love in Sweetwater County

A Sugar Maple Holiday Novel

(Historical)

If You Keep Me

If You Choose Me

A Sugar Maple Novel

If You Love Me

If You Adore Me

If You Cherish Me

If You Hold Me

If You Kiss Me

Riverbend

In All My Wishes

In All My Years

In All My Dreams

In All My Life

A Christmas Spark

A Miracle Mountain Christmas

HISTORICAL WESTERNS:

McKinnie Mail Order Brides Series

Love on the Prairie

(USA Today Bestselling Novel)

Love in the Rockies

Love on the Plains

Love on the Ranch

His Holiday Promise

(A Love on the Ranch Novella)

Love on the Sound

Love on the Border

(Coming April 2021)

Love at the Coast

A Prospectors Novel

Fools Rush

Bride of America

Adelaide: Bride of Maryland

ABOUT THE AUTHOR

Ciara Knight is a USA TODAY Bestselling Author, who writes clean and wholesome romance novels set in either modern day small towns or wild historic old west. Born with a huge imagination that usually got her into trouble, Ciara is happy she's found a way to use her powers for good. She loves spending time with her characters and hopes you do, too.

Made in the USA
Columbia, SC
12 October 2022